T0165568

Squeaky

A BLACK CAT'S TALE

Stephanie R. Aivaz

SQUEAKY
A BLACK CAT'S TALE

Copyright © 2016 Stephanie R. Aivaz.

All rights reserved. No part of this book may be used or reproduced by any means, graphic, electronic, or mechanical, including photocopying, recording, taping or by any information storage retrieval system without the written permission of the author except in the case of brief quotations embodied in critical articles and reviews.

This is a work of fiction. All of the characters, names, incidents, organizations, and dialogue in this novel are either the products of the author's imagination or are used fictitiously.

iUniverse books may be ordered through booksellers or by contacting:

iUniverse
1663 Liberty Drive
Bloomington, IN 47403
www.iuniverse.com
1-800-Authors (1-800-288-4677)

Because of the dynamic nature of the Internet, any web addresses or links contained in this book may have changed since publication and may no longer be valid. The views expressed in this work are solely those of the author and do not necessarily reflect the views of the publisher, and the publisher hereby disclaims any responsibility for them.

Any people depicted in stock imagery provided by Thinkstock are models, and such images are being used for illustrative purposes only. Certain stock imagery © Thinkstock.

ISBN: 978-1-4917-9397-8 (sc)
ISBN: 978-1-4917-9398-5 (e)

Library of Congress Control Number: 2016905751

Print information available on the last page.

iUniverse rev. date: 5/4/2016

I want to thank my family for believing in me, for nudging me, yelling at me, laughing with me, and just putting up with me through this journey. Sharing with those close to me is easy, but sharing with the world is a whole other ball game. Even though fiction, a book reflects the inner self of its author. The writing and imagination was easy. The revealing of the inner self was very difficult.

Thank you, Susan Schindler, for your expertise in grammar editing, Dominic Fauci for your artwork, and my Joe. Without you and all my children, this dream would never have been fulfilled.

Part I

Babyhood

Chapter 1

I was born in the small city of Kingston, New York, located in the Hudson Valley region, close to the Hudson River. My first recollections were of suckling my mama's soft teats and drinking that luscious warm mother's milk. I had four other siblings, well actually five, but one, my mama totally rejected and it died. She didn't leave it lie in our den, but carried it away somewhere, then came to lay down with us so we could snuggle around her warm belly and sleep.

Our den was under the porch of a house in the city. Lots of noises and acrid smells outside, which I later came to find out, were automobiles and people. But, it was dark and warm and had the sweet smell of dirt and my mama in our den. Mama used to carry us one by one over to a corner of the den and tell us this is where to potty. Never to go to the bathroom anywhere else in our home. She'd patiently wait for us to go, and then carry us back one by one to our bed. She would go back and dig a hole and cover our entire potty. Then she would come back and lie with us, cleaning us all up. Oh that warm rough tongue. Sometimes we didn't want to be cleaned. We'd squirm and wiggle to get away from it, but she would sigh with that motherly patience and tell us to lie still and be good. Clean is an important part of your life.

Once in a while she would go to hunt food for herself. Oh those were scary times. No warm mama and our bellies would get hungry. The five of us would huddle and see monsters in the corners of our den. We'd cry and cry. Please come home mama. And she did come home. We'd see her squeeze through the hole in the porch fencing and we'd squeal with happiness. Our little bodies would wiggle like crazy. She'd curl up around us and tell us to be quiet. Cats should always be very quiet she'd say. "No one must know you are around. Humans can be mean and they will kill us. So hush up."

We'd finally settle down, but she would stay very alert, listening for anything that was different for the longest time. Then she would let herself sleep for a while.

Mama was what humans call a feral cat. She had no owner, no house to go home to, no food dish, and no water. She roamed the streets digging in garbage cans for leftovers, catching small rodents and an occasional snake, drinking from rain puddles and making do with whatever was available. She never had a permanent home. Only when she was ready to have a litter did she find a place that she could nest and keep her children safe. Mama wasn't that old either. Only around four or so. We were her sixth litter and she was a very good mother. Mama was worn though. Her life wasn't an easy one living on the streets, and having so many children was weakening her body and health. She was a fierce protector of her children. She'd give life and limb to protect us and we always felt safe with her.

One night, I came awake with mama in a very alert and angry mood, hissing at the darkness. She had drawn us under her, with haunches ready to pounce, hair raised, whiskers quivering, teeth showing and claws fully extended. Over her hissing I heard a slithering, rustling sound. I peeked out from under her and saw two red dots glowing in the darkness. Sniffing the air, I smelled a dank and sour odor. Scared me terribly. I pulled myself back under mama and tried to find her teat, whining and complaining the whole time. "Shush" she said.

She started to growl. A low guttural growl which vibrated above us like a freight train rumbling through. Made my fear even worse and my three sisters and I climbed into such a tight ball that one probably thought we were one ball of fur. We shivered and cried for what seemed like forever, and then mama flew up on her hind legs and hit the red dots with lightening speed and force. There was a great thump and hissing of another nature. The red dots flew up in the air and hit the ground and disappeared into the darkness under the house. Mama watched the dark for a few seconds and came back to us. She had that terrible rank odor on her that emanated from the red dots, which made us all feel terrified.

"Rats, I hate rats", she said as she started cleaning that smell from her body. Once done with herself she started cleaning us and let us feed. "Children," she warned, "rats are dangerous. They can carry a disease that would make us very ill, and they will try and steal you and kill you. Don't have anything to do with them."

From the darkness, we heard the rustling noises again, and a hissing whisper that said, "Baby cat, baby cat, oh so good to eat. I'll have my meal yet my pretty."

Then and there, mamma said we were going to move. "Our nest is not safe anymore. We must find another."

One by one she picked us up and carried us out through her hole in the fencing, placing us in the darkest corner of the lawn by the steps. The air was different. It was cooler and the wind was starting to blow. It brought with it so many different smells. Some were so good they brought a yearning to my tummy for something I didn't understand, and others burned my eyes and throat.

Out here the noises were much louder and when a car passed, I was astonished and so frightened, it was probably the first time in my life I was speechless. Mama said to calm down and pay close attention to what she was going to say.

"I have to find a safe place for us to live. I am going to look for that place and will be back shortly. I want you to stay together and make no noise and no shenanigans. Even if you get hungry or scared. No noise. Do you understand? I can't stress to you how important this is." And off she went into the darkness.

We were only about two weeks old. Just being able to see was a brand new experience. We were still unsteady on our feet and really didn't understand much at all. We understood survival though. So, we balled up together and even I didn't make a peep. We waited for what seemed like an eternity and boy was I hungry and I had to pee really badly. Mama said not to move and it was bad to tinkle where I lay, so I held it. Besides that, the evil smell was back again. Not as close, but I could smell it. Just as I thought I was going to explode, we heard mamma coming back. She checked us all over and let us feed a little and potty before she told us her plan.

She said she had a place to take us, but could only take one at a time, so we must stay quiet and still until she had all of us in our new home. Mama picked me up first by the back of my neck and off we went. We went across the sidewalk, under a fence, across a lawn and into a garage, up a set of steps into a loft area, and she placed me behind a big box that smelled good. I was talking up a storm about the bad smell back at our old home, but she told me not to squeak so much. Then off she went, returning three times, and dropping my sisters down next to me. The fourth time she was gone a long time. I started to whine and my sisters picked up on my act. We cried and cried.

Mama came limping back a long time later with that bad smell on her body. She lay down next to us and I sensed she was sobbing. Quiet, but deep anguish filled sadness came from her belly and she had tears in her eyes. My fourth sister wasn't with her. She let us feed, while cleaning the wounds on her body. Once our bellies we full, we were wondering where our sister was. While mamma cleaned us she told us what happened.

"On my last trip back, I smelled the evil rat even from a distance. He must have followed us as we went through the hole, just waiting for his chance. This time he had more of his kind with him."

Mamma heard our sister screaming and ran as fast as she could back to her, but it was too late. The rats had ganged up on her little baby and she was dead before mamma could do anything to help her. "I took revenge though. Tore holes in the bellies of at least four of them, if not more. Ripped an ear off one and broke the leg of another. Rats don't heal, so they will slink off and die."

But she paid a price. There were several gashes around her head and neck and she was limping badly. She groaned in pain whenever she moved her one front leg.

She went on to tell us that she carried my sister half way back and laid her down on some soft sweet smelling grass. Then she came home to us. Finally she fell into an exhausted sleep and we snuggled down on her warm body for the rest of the night.

We didn't understand the meaning of death and our sister not being there was forgotten almost overnight. As young as we were, our main concern was food and warmth. What we did respond to as infants was the feelings that came from mama. Her feelings were teaching us to respond in the world so that we could survive. So, when we woke up and mama was slow to respond, we nudged something awful. It was time to eat and then potty.

# Chapter 2

Mama growled that morning and was very short tempered with us. I could feel the remorse of her loss and it was not a good feeling. I acknowledged in my mind the pain she woke up with, but could not understand it. All her gentleness seemed to be shrouded in this pain and sadness. But, she finally did get up and take us down the stairs one at a time to a corner of the yard. The pre-dawn light lent different smells to the outside. The sweet fragrances coming from the earth were amazing. Having to walk on the grass wet with dew was an experience in itself. It felt funny and kind of spongy, making my feet itchy. The grass tickled my belly and made me want to giggle. One thing I didn't like was the thought of pottying on the wet grass, so I tried pushing it aside before I squatted. Then I didn't like that smell after I went to the bathroom, so I tried to scratch the grass back over it. Mama came up and smiled at me. "What a big boy you are trying to be."

I lay down on the grass and rolled over and over. What a delightful feeling. Then, I really looked at her and she was a mess. Chunks of her hair were missing and she had a big gash on her neck, her ear was torn and another spot on her forehead was open and oozing a metallic raw meat type of odor. Her left front leg had a big bite in it also, making her wince every time she put weight on it. Poor mama I thought and I started to cry.

"Hush my noisy one," she said, lifting me up off the ground and carrying me back into the garage and up the stairs to our new nest.

After she had us all back up there, she lay down and while we fed, she licked her wounds. Mama slept most of that day away and we laid there with her listening to all the outside noises. I sniffed the air a few times checking for that evil smell. Nothing there and I would fall back to sleep, only to wake up and sniff the air again.

These were my first recollections of my life. The garage that I spent my babyhood in was a great place to grow up. We actually had our own door. Mama got us in and out of there through the back of the garage. There was a loose plank in the back wall. Pushing gently there was room enough for her to get us through. Then we went up the stairs where our nest was, and where the humans stored a lot of unused stuff.

In the first couple of weeks, there was plenty of food for mama. Little mice roamed all over the place. She didn't have to go far from us to catch her meal. This was a good thing because she limped quite a bit and couldn't jump like she'd done before. She seemed to take forever to heal, but heal she did. She always continued to limp slightly after her fight, especially when the weather was rainy. She slept a lot the first week after the rats, and moaned in her sleep, but slowly, with continuous care, her wounds healed without infection.

As we reached five weeks, we became more and more curious about our surroundings. We had so many things to check out in our loft. Boxes full of things. My sisters and I got one open and in it was full of soft clothes humans wear. We pulled everything out of that box and pulled it all over the floor. It was a delight, scratching the material, rolling in it, even chewing some buttons off and then playing, batting them around. We had so much fun.

Mama came back from a hunting trip one day carrying a snake. "Look what I caught for you children."

We looked at it. We smelled it; we whacked it with our paws, and then asked her what do we do with it? "You eat it of course. Its food," she said, with a giggle in her voice. "It's time you starting eating solid food."

Well, I thought as I sat down and stared at this thing, "I don't think so. Mama's milk is what I'll have."

I ran under her and tried to suckle, but she gently pushed me away. "No, it's time to learn how to eat other things."

My sisters looked at her with terror in their eyes. "We'll starve," they whined in unison. Mama laughed at this and told us with a firm note in her voice that we would not get any milk until we tried eating some snake.

I turned my back on her and stalked off to another spot in the loft. My sisters on the other hand, looked at one another and decided to try it. Mama lay down and watched, glancing every once in a while in my direction with a smile on her face. My sisters dug in, making all these chewy noises and then these yummy to my tummy noises.

"What's so good about that?" I thought, as I peeked at them.

I inched my way over to where they were eating and sniffed. "Not a bad smell. Sort of meaty and fresh. Sort of like the metallic raw smell of mama's cuts only different," is what I thought as my tummy grumbled.

I glanced at mama and nuzzled my way over to her belly. She pushed me away saying I must try some. "Okay, just a little taste mama."

I pushed in between my sisters, pulled a small piece close to me with my claws, closed my eyes and tasted. It was different. It was chewy and it was oh so good. I dug in with the girls and ate until my belly was full. From that day forward, I decided snake was the best tasting food, next to mama's milk, in whole the world.

Chapter 3

I remember when I discovered I had a tail. I was crouched down in the early evening's warm grass, watching a butterfly, and this thing kept swishing behind me.

"What in the world is that?" I rolled over on my belly and grabbed it, pulled it up to my mouth and took a bite. "Ouch, that hurt. It bit me back."

I jumped up and started chasing it, around and around in a circle, yelling "stop, stop." I got so tired, I had to sit down and catch my breath. That thing kept eluding me. I just couldn't quite latch on to it. Mama was sitting in the shade by our door watching me, always on the alert.

She started to giggle. "Oh, my noisy, squeaky little one, you are so funny at times."

I ran over to her for protection and that damn thing followed me. It cuddled up next to mama just like it belonged there. Made me really angry, so I reached down and bit it again, and it bit me back again. This time I was so frustrated I started to cry. "Shush, my silly boy," mama said. She leaned down and started cleaning me. "That is your tail. It belongs to you."

"Belongs to me?" I asked. "What do I do with it?"

Mama sighed with a smile on her face. "It is attached to you and helps you keep your balance, fluffs up when your adrenalin pumps in battle, making you look huge, chases the bugs away.

The tail does hundreds of things. Nature gave it to you for a reason. It's a good thing."

I still kept an eye on that tail for several days after, just checking to make sure it wasn't something that was following me. Chased it and bit it every once in a while to test mama's story. I wasn't so sure that it was suppose to be there all the time at all.

Chapter 4

One morning, when mama was busy teaching us how to hunt mice up in our nest, I sneaked out. I felt antsy that day and a little rebellious. There was so much to see out in the garden. She was busy with my sisters who were very good students and everything mama told them, they took as law. Me, I questioned everything, all the time. Mama would get frustrated with me, but said it was because I was male. Someday, I would decide to leave the nest and brave the world on my own. Once that day came, I would never return.

Naturally, I questioned that too, but right now, I had a home to come back too and a very inquisitive mind.

Bouncing out into my garden, I stopped and picked up on a strange noise coming from the yard by the house where I was told never to go in daylight. I crouched down and slowly inched my way around the side of the garage, with the grass tickling my belly. Inch by inch I crawled with my whiskers twitching, ears back, and every hair on my body seemed to sense the air. I peaked around the front of the garage. There sitting on the back steps of the house, talking to a tiny plastic thing, was a little human. I sniffed and sniffed and could pick up no danger signals. I inched more and more out into the yard. I watched and watched, fascinated by this little human. "It must be a child like mama calls me and it smells female. Gentle odors of fresh water and happiness. No evil foul smells like mama warned me humans have."

"What should I do? This little human felt safe. I wonder what she would do if I just walked up to her and said hello? Mama said humans would hurt us and chase us, but I'm fast. I've got a tail that makes me look huge when the adrenalin is pumping and I'm male. Makes me very strong."

I think I debated a long time, but my curiosity got in the way. I got up and marched half way across the lawn and suddenly she looked up, stopped talking to that plastic thing and stared straight at me. My legs got weak and I plopped down. "What did I do?" I thought. "I'm in trouble now. Big trouble." All my brave thoughts went away and all I could think of is what mama told me about humans.

Instead she smiled, put the plastic thing down on the step, and said, "A kitty cat. A little baby kitty cat. Hello kitten. Where did you come from?"

She was amazing. Not at all mean like mama said they were. And she didn't chase me either. Instead she put out one of her paws and called to me. I sniffed and sniffed and slowly made my way over to her. I sat down just out of reach, mainly because my legs were still shaking and I thought I might just flop down like a dumb bunny. "Damn," I thought, there goes that tail swishing again. "Not now stupid."

She stretched forward and I backed up a bit. "It's just my hand silly," she said. " I won't hurt you. Where did you come from?"

Then it hit me. "How do I know what she's saying to me? Her voice makes these weird sounds, but I understand them. I feel, smell and understand them." So I answered her. "I live with my mama and my sisters and mama says I'm noisy and male."

All she heard was "meow, meow."

"Silly black kitty she said, you are so pretty. Pretty black kitty. I'll call you Blackie. Can I pet you?" She reached out. I stretched my neck a little and let her touch me.

"Yeow," what a feeling. Her hand laid itself on my back and I felt this tingling feeling up and down my spine. "What a nice feeling." I jumped up and did a dance. My tail stood straight up and twitched around. "How dare you take any credit for this happy feeling tail," and I proceeded to grab it and bite it.

The little girl human giggled and laughed. "My precious Blackie."

With that, a big female human came out of the door of the house. "What are you laughing about Amanda? You sound so happy. Oh, a kitten," she said, as she looked down at me.

Well, talk about frightened. I was terrified. "What had I done? Now I'll be dead stew meat for sure." I was frozen. My legs wouldn't move and my heart pumped so bad I thought it would pop out.

"It's just a baby" the big human said. "Where did it come from?"

"Its name is Blackie, and it came from the garden."

With that I got the strength in my legs back and bolted for the garage. "Oh mama is going to be mad at me." as I raced as fast as I could for safety.

Chapter 5

Once around the corner of the garage, I stopped and peeked out. The little girl looked sad, and the big mama human, was talking to her soothingly. "It's okay Amanda. We will leave a bowl of milk out for it. Blackie will come back again, and we will talk to daddy."

I watched and listened some more, but the little girl and her mother went into the house. I lay down in the grass for a while listening to my heart beat and thinking about what I had done. "I'd better not tell mama or my sisters." Then I started thinking about how I knew what they were saying. The little girl didn't understand me, I sensed that, but I could understand her. "This is something I have to figure out."

With that thought, I heard mama calling me. "Where is my squeaky boy?"

"I'm right here mama, just checking out downstairs", as I ran up to the loft.

"You're such a wanderer. You'll have all your adult life to travel, so don't make me worry all the time now."

That night as we all cuddled together, cleaning ourselves and one another, I started thinking about being a black cat. I even had a name, Blackie. I was warm and content and thought that mama might understand. I just couldn't fall asleep until I shared. "Mama, I'm a black cat ..."

"What did you say?" She was suddenly alert, and looking quite angry.

"I said I'm a black cat and my name is Blackie", I mewed more afraid not to repeat my statement than to keep quiet.

"Where did you get that from?" she hissed as she rapped me with her paw.

"I, uh, I spoke to the little girl who lives in the house. She said I was a black cat and my name is Blackie. She was nice mama. She didn't chase me, or hurt me or anything like that. She wants to be my friend."

"Friend my ass," she hissed, mad as hell at me. "Did she follow you home? Answer me my suddenly speechless one. Does she know where we live?"

I knew I shouldn't have said anything. "No mama, no. I was smart and ran away towards the other yard when the big human lady came out. The grass was real tall and I disappeared in it quickly. When they went in, I came home."

Mama lay down again, with a great big sigh and didn't speak to me all night. I lay off to the side away from her and my sisters, afraid she might hit me again. "I shouldn't have told her."

The next day was a very rainy one, very dark and dreary with thunder and lightening. Mama always said to stay in the nest when the weather got like this, so we all just hung out. My sisters were ignoring me also. They wrestled and chased one another, played in the old clothes, chased buttons and napped.

Mama was lying there half snoozing and half watching my sisters play. Finally she looked at me and said, "Come over here my troublemaker. I have a story to tell you."

I crawled over to her expecting another blow, but she was gentle and loving like she always was. I nursed a bit, and she nuzzled me. I knew all would be good again.

Chapter 6

Mama cat had wrestled with the dilemma of how to handle the situation her son had gotten them into. The kittens were getting older and it would soon be time to leave the nest completely. She knew the girls would probably stay near by and she would see them once in a great while, but her son would leave never to return. He, by nature, would be the wanderer and she'd never see him again once he left the security of his den. With this in mind, she had decided to tell him her story.

"I lived with humans once," she chirped.

She totally caught me off guard. I looked at her with astonishment. "You did? And I'm really black? What color are you?"

Mama chuckled. "You are black in color and most likely take after your father. I'm what they call a dark gray tabby and so is one of your sisters. The other two are gray and white. Now back to my story."

"My mama is a house cat. She lives with a nice family down the street. When she was just a teenager, she came into heat. Of course a big old Tom cat smelled her and came courting. At first, she was terrified of him, but he was persistent, coming to the house every day and every night, mewling his affection for her. As the days passed, the urge to be with him grew greater and greater until one morning when the kids were going out the door she bolted past them, down the stairs and around to the yard. She couldn't stop herself. There he was waiting for her, handsome and so pleasant. She took off with him into the high grasses and disappeared. The family was in an uproar and very upset. The children cried, and the mother human searched all over for her to no avail. My mother took off with that big old Tom for two days, making love over and over."

On the third morning she woke up and he was gone. She was sore, hungry and confused, and wondering why she ever did such a thing.

Getting her bearings, she finally found her house, climbed the stairs and waited at the front door until one of the children found her. She went in and slept for almost two days. After a week or so she became so hungry she would do nothing but eat and was getting fatter and fatter. Sure enough she was pregnant and gave birth to four kittens in a toy box under the bed of her favorite little person. I was one of those four.

The human family didn't seem terribly upset, but didn't want all these cats in the house. They took us and mama to the animal doctor. We all got shots and mama was what they called fixed.

When we were about six weeks old, the humans took us in our toy box to a very noisy smelly place where there were so many other humans. They put a sign on the box that said "free kittens." One by one we were taken away from mama. I never saw my brothers and sister again. A very nice, but old, lady took me home with her.

I could smell the old on her and knew she wasn't well. I was terrified that first week and hardly came out from under her couch except when I had to go to the bathroom so bad I had to use the potty box, or if I was so hungry I had to eat. The food was okay and my potty box was always clean. She would talk to me constantly and I realized I knew what she was saying. I felt her words and knew she was kind and was going to be good to me. She bought me toys and brushed me and treated me wonderful. I'd lay in her lap while she stroked me and I was content except for the smell of sickness on her. That made me feel sad. Life was good for a while. Then the smell of sickness grew stronger. My mistress cried a lot and was getting weaker and weaker. Sometimes she would forget to feed me and oftentimes my litter box would stay dirty. One day another, younger lady showed up and moved in with us. She was nice and made sure my box was clean and my food dish was full. She was there taking care of my person and I learned that this was my mistress' daughter. Then, like my mother before me, I went into heat. Did the same thing my mama did and returned three days later, tired and hungry. To my surprise there was another human in the house. It was a male who smelled vile and did not like me in the least.

All he did was complain about the old lady and her cat living in his house. The younger lady often corrected him saying this was her mother's house and her mother's cat. If he didn't like it, he should leave. He'd snort, grumble and go sit in the living room and watch television. He liked to kick me, so I stayed out of his way, mostly upstairs with my mistress who was in bed all of the time now.

Just like my mother before me, I grew fat and lazy for a while, staying in my mistress's room most of the time except to potty and eat. I sensed her daughter was afraid the male would hurt me, and scooted me out of harm's way when he came home. Then I started to worry. I knew my time was near. Where could I have my babies that would be safe? I prowled the house looking for a place away from his smell. I finally decided on a dark corner in the basement. When my time came, I found an old musty smelling blanket sitting high up on a work table. I dragged it down, made myself comfortable and gave birth to my first litter.

There were six babies, three boys, three girls, one more beautiful than the other. I was oh so nervous and kept thinking, "what if I'm not a good mother?" But my natural instincts kicked in and I knew exactly what to do. I cleaned them up, and let them nurse. I knew I was going to be a good mother and never felt happier in my whole life. This happiness was not meant to be.

I stayed with my babies for about a day and a half before hunger and thirst set in. I knew that in order to keep them healthy, I had to keep myself well nourished. I went upstairs to the kitchen to where my food and water dishes were. He was in the kitchen getting something out of the big cold box humans call a refrigerator. He looked down at me and said, "Here's the old lady's rat. Where have you been? Driving the old dame nuts and having my wife looking all over kingdom come for you."

He bent down to pick me up and I hissed and scratched as if my life depended on it. He dropped me cursing and yelling. I flew back down the stairs of the basement over to my nest and curled up around my babies, shaking like a leaf. He followed me down and found us.

I remember thinking that I was a bad mother. I should never have run to my babies. I should have gone upstairs and away from them. Looking back, I guess it was because I was so young, not more then a kitten myself and I went to them for the warmth, security and happiness they gave me.

The man looked down at us turned around and walked away. I thought, "that was a close call." Now I had to move us somewhere else. That was my last sane thought for a long time. He came back right away carrying a plastic bag, knocked me out of the way and started putting my babies in the bag. I screamed and attacked him.

I scratched and bit and fought with all my strength, but he was too big for me. He whacked me in the head and I spun across the floor, stunned. By the time I got my wind back he was heading up the stairs with my babies. I flew up after him and grabbed his leg with my front claws and teeth. I arched my body and raked as hard as I could with my back claws.

He cursed at me, put the bag down and reached for me, pulled me off of him by the back of my neck and threw me across the kitchen floor. Grabbing the bag he went outside leaving the door slightly open and growling like a wounded rat.

He hurt me this time pretty bad. I had an awful time just getting up on all fours. I crawled to the door and down the outside steps and just laid there for what seemed like an eternity, trying to overcome the pain in my side. I must have been panting quite loudly because he heard me. He watched me the whole time with what I swore was an evil grin while he got a garbage can, and put the plastic bag with my babies in it. Then he took the garden hose, turned it on and started to fill the can full of water. He then put the top on the can and walked off.

I heard my babies screaming for help. I got up and with all the strength I had left, I charged the can, I clawed, I begged, I screamed. I could do nothing but listen to my little ones' cries get fainter and fainter until there was nothing but quiet. I knew they were gone. I wanted to die too. I crawled off into the tall grass by the fence and laid there sobbing for a long time.

I must have passed out, because the next thing I remember it was dark and raining. As I gained consciousness, my whole body started to throb. I was one giant ache and started thinking that my babies must be hungry. Then I remembered what happened and cried some more. It rained most of that night and I laid there drenched, with the rain cleaning my bloody body. I was very dehydrated and weak from what I had been through, but the rain gave me something to drink.

I never went back to that house. Early morning brought the garbage truck and my babies went away in it. I watched and said goodbye, and then limped away. I wandered for a long time, sleeping wherever I could find shelter. I ate bugs, went through garbage cans and was always hungry. I learned how to hunt out of necessity. My mother never had to hunt for survival, so I never learned from her, but instinct finally prevailed and I got better and better. As I ate more, I got healthy again and I went into heat. You children are my newest litter of babies. I've never trusted humans again, and have never lost a litter since."

"Mama that is very sad. Why would someone be so mean?"

"Because, my squeaky one, that is the way humans are. Its how the mood strikes them. There are nice ones and evil ones, but in the long run, nothing good comes of a relationship with humans. I told you my story because you will leave this home forever someday soon. You will have many a den, but never a nest simply because you are male. Your roaming of your territory and protection of your females will be your greatest concern and many a battle will be fought with other males who would like to take your harem. If you lived with a kind human, they would not be able to stop you from roaming and will tire of you quickly. You will have a difficult life and I don't want to see you complicate it with humans."

I thought about what mama had shared with me. Even though I didn't quite understand the depth of all she told me, I knew someday I would grow up and be like her Tom. This I understood instinctively. I knew I had better pay more attention to my hunting lessons and less time playing. I would be a good cat from now on in and stay away from the humans.

Chapter 7

It rained heavily for a couple of days, so we did not venture out. I was a very studious boy those couple of days, paying attention to everything mama was teaching us. She kept sniffing me to see if I was feeling well. Assured that I was fine, she went on with our lessons, glancing at me when I wasn't looking trying to figure out what I was thinking.

Sometime in the night the rain stopped and the early morning air brought with it fresh green smells and a hint of something else. There was a slightly different odor to the trees and bushes. More sharp and crisp then before. I scooted out our door when everyone else was asleep just to roll around in the wet warm grass. Just as I sat up and started drying myself, I sensed a rustling in the shadows of the hedge. Totally alert, ears pricked back to pick up more of the sound, I spotted a lazy movement slipping along. "Wow, a snake."

I started to turn and call for mama. "Wait a minute," I thought. "This is my opportunity to show her how well I can hunt."

I lay down perfectly still with whiskers at full attention moving with the sound. Whiskers are perfect sensors. I could feel every movement the snake made and knew he wasn't aware of me yet. Closer and closer he slithered. My muscles tensed and I positioned myself and then pounced. My hind muscles springing me forward, I landed on my front paws, claws fully extended and hit the snake just behind his neck. I brought my head down, fangs gleaming and bit, severing his spine. Then I picked him up, dragging the snake's body along under my belly, and strutted back to mama and my sisters. Mama was so proud of me and I just was full of myself all morning. "Ha," I said to my sisters, "whose better then me?" I stuffed my belly and fell into a deep sleep next to mama and dreamed of my first big kill.

I woke up abruptly from my sleep feeling as if something was calling to me. As I became more alert, I heard the distinctive voice of the little girl calling out "Blackie, Blackie, where are you?"

Jumping up, I sniffed mama and my sisters. They were still asleep enjoying the fullness of my kill. With lightening speed, I ran down the stairs and out our door. Pulling myself up sharply, I remembered what mama had told me about humans, so I sat down for a minute to think the situation over and a butterfly caught my attention. It was flipping in and out of the long weeds, fluttering just above my head. I forgot about what I was thinking about, and jumped up and snapped at it. I missed and started prancing around in circles trying to catch it, when suddenly I realized I had danced all the way into the back yard. I heard a gleeful, "There you are Blackie. I knew you would come back."

It was the little girl. I could sense how happy she was to see me. "Oh, boy," I thought, "what am I suppose to do? Mama said humans are dangerous, but her circumstances were different. This little girl thinks I'm the greatest and she smells good too."

Playing with her for a little while wouldn't hurt anything. Cautiously, I walked towards the little girl, tail straight up in the air, just strutting my stuff.

The little girl squatted down and put her hand out. "Hi ya Blackie, can I pet you?"

I stretched my neck and sniffed the little girl's hand. "Oh it smelled so good, like special food and grass and rain and sunshine." I felt so suddenly happy that I did a dance and the little girl laughed.

She stood up and turned towards the house. "I have something special for you to eat Blackie. Come on, you must be hungry." She walked back toward the back porch of the house and I followed. At a fair distance mind you, but I followed just enthralled with the little girl.

Once she was up on the porch she picked up a bowl with white stuff in it, and placed it in the grass at the bottom of the stairs. "This is for you," she said. "It's milk. Nice and cold. You must be thirsty."

I stretched and sniffed, whiskers going a mile a minute. I pulled back, stretched and sniffed again. "This stuff smells good, like mama's milk, only different, stronger, and more pungent." Tentatively I moved towards the dish, and finally curiosity overcame me and I licked some up. "Meowwwww, that's different." It was cold like the rain, sweet like mama's milk, but stronger tasting.

The little girl got the giggles, pointing at me she said, "You've got milk all over your face like a white mask."

I made a face and thought "how embarrassing," then sat down and started to clean it off with my paw, completely forgetting how close the little girl was. She slid into the grass beside me and started to stroke my back, sing songing my name over and over.

"Oh, it felt sooooo good" I mewed. "How about my belly?" laying down and rolling over, exposing a bikini patch of white on my lower belly.

Then I heard my mama call. I jumped up, spun around and took off towards the garage. "Blackie don't go, please don't go," the little girl wailed, and I could feel her sadness.

I stopped and went back to her, rubbed my body along her legs tickling her nose with the tip of my tail. "I'll be back little girl, I promise. I like you too."

The words came out in a chirping sound, and the little girl seemed to understand me. "Please come back soon and stay with me."

Chapter 8

"My son, I am so angry with you. I bared my soul to you. I tried to pound into your head that humans are dangerous, and what do you do? You let one pet you and feed you. You make friends with one." She growled and growled for what seem like forever to me.

"Mama, I like her. She is my friend and I feel something special coming from her. She'll never hurt me. I have a name too. It's Blackie from now on."

"I will never call you by a human given name", she hissed and stalked off into the shadows of the garage.

I figured she would get over it. She did before, so I curled up in our sleeping place waiting for my sisters and mama to come back. I fell asleep and dreamed of the evil human mama had known. I started crying in my sleep and felt like I was fighting for my life, paws and legs flailing, claws coming out and retracting. I finally woke up feeling exhausted and noticed it was dark. Mama and my sisters were not back yet. I sniffed the air and fully extended my whiskers to sense the air and track their movements. There wasn't any. They were not there. At first I thought they may have gone outside, so I ran down the stairs calling to them. Out into the night I flew yelling for them. Nothing. They were gone. Only the remnants of their odors remained. Suddenly I knew. I was alone in the world now. Just like mama said would happen. I lay down in the grass and sobbed, "Please mama come back for me. Please come back."

Finally I got up and looked around. I was somewhat frustrated with the loneliness and sudden emptiness I felt and had to go to the bathroom so bad, so I sniffed around looking for a spot. Instead of squatting like I normally did, I stuck my tail high in the air and sprayed my scent all over the high grass. What a great feeling. It released the tension that had built up inside of me. "I could do this forever," I yelled out, but eventually no more would come out.

I snorted and looked behind me. So much of the grass was wet and shiny in the starlight. I had to go back and sniff to make sure it was I that had wet the grass so much. Once I had established this, I stalked off towards the garage.

Laying there by myself, the solitude really kicked in, and I mewed my sadness to the quiet, empty garage.

Mama had not totally abandoned him. She mulled over in her mind what was happening and decided it was just a matter of time before the humans realized where the nest was. She was bound and determined never to become controlled by another human again. Blackie, as he now called himself, had made a decision. He had become friends with the little girl when he was told not to. Her charges were getting older now, almost 8 weeks. In another 4 weeks or so, her girls would be old enough to fend for themselves. Mama knew she would probably go into heat again and the urge would overcome her and she would take off with her Tom to start another litter. Then the girls would be moving on to their own destinies. She'd have to chase her son away then because males were dangerous to have around kittens and especially around sisters heading into heat. How she knew this she didn't know, but only knew that it was best in nature if he did leave.

He was still young enough to be under her charge and her motherly instincts would not let her abandon him yet.

Mama had gathered the girls and told them that they would be looking for a new den to live in and not to ask any questions. Their brother would be staying to guard the old nest for awhile. So, while he was sleeping, they, quietly as shadows, followed mama out into the yard. "You are old enough to help me find a new place now," she said. "Be brave and help me search." Finally, after several hours of roaming the neighborhood, they found an old abandoned wooden utility shed. It smelled of oil and machinery and dirt. It had a great vegetable garden right next to it full of tomato plants, peppers and squash. On the other side of the garden was a newer shed full of the equipment used for gardening. Mama sniffed and smelled. Except for the smell of mice and cow manure, there was no other animal smells. "This will do well," mama told the girls. "We must be very quiet and stay out of sight when the humans come to get their vegetables."

The girls didn't particularly like it as much as the loft, but mama had spoken and they never argued with her.

After mama helped them make themselves comfortable, she nursed them. Something she didn't do too often anymore, but she needed to give them the warmth and security they needed. Once they were warm, full and content, mama said, "I want you to stay put until I return. I'm going back to check on your brother."

She still limped and was not as fast on her feet as she once was. She needed the girls help as they searched for their new den, but now, traveling to check on her son, was something she needed to do alone.

Mama went back to the garage and quietly checked the nest. Blackie was lying there mewling his loneliness. She lay down quietly in the shadows and watched.

Ordinarily, even though I was still a kitten, I would have sensed another cat and picked up on the smell. But mama's smell was all over the nest and she lay so still, I did not feel any movement.

Finally I got up and stretched my body, extended my claws, and yawned a big yawn. I was getting hungry and there was nothing to eat. I pranced down the stairs and out into the yard smelling and sniffing the air.

I caught the whiff of something good coming from the back porch of the house. Stalking the scent, I cautiously walked over to the back steps and up onto the deck. There were two bowls sitting out in the starlight. One was familiar. It was the scent of the white stuff I had tasted earlier in the day. The other was different. "Ummm, it's some kind of food. It's not mouse or snake, but smells something like animal. The odor is not as strong as blood, but definitely edible." I slowly stepped toward it, ears back listening behind me, whiskers twitching, and my muscles ready to take flight in an instant. I looked around and checked the air. Nothing to be alarmed about I thought. Tentatively I tasted the animal smelling stuff. It was crunchy and as I chewed it, its flavor got better and better. Once more I checked the air for danger. Not feeling any, I sat down and ate. I finished the whole dish full of food and then washed it down with some of the white stuff. "Oh boy" I thought, "if only my mama and sisters were here to enjoy this. I'd share with them."

I stretched a long stretch, and then sat down to clean myself. Out of the corner of my eye I caught movement. I perked up, lifting my body up into fight or flight mode and sniffed the air. Whatever it was it was going away and did not pose any danger. I sat down again and started to scratch my ears and back with my hind leg. Then I buried my nose into my side and scratched with my teeth. I was so itchy lately; it was even waking me up from my sleep.

The movement Blackie saw was his mama leaving. She knew that he was going to become a house cat and live with the humans. This was not what she had wanted for her special squeaky little boy, but this was what he was choosing. Off into the night she went, knowing that her job was done. She'd miss this precious one, but he chose his path.

Part II

Childhood

Chapter 9

I didn't go back to the garage that night. My belly was full, I felt no danger around, so I curled up in a dark corner of the porch and fell asleep. I woke often, scratching the damn itches, and could smell the essence of the little girl, giving me a warm fuzzy.

The next morning, the little girl was out the door early calling for me. I stretched out, walked from my corner and rubbed against her legs, tickling her thigh with my tail.

She was thrilled I was there and bent down to pet me. Again, the lush feeling of happiness swarmed over me, when all of a sudden I was going up in the air. my legs went out and I started scratching at the air.

"Oh stop it Blackie", the little girl said, "I won't hurt you. I just want to look at you."

She cradled me in her arms and ran into the house yelling for her mama. "Look who came back mama, my Blackie!"

Mama looked down and said "Well, well Amanda, I guess we have a pet." She took me from Amanda and up I went even higher in the air. Oh, I was getting sick to my stomach.

Amanda's Mama said, "It looks to be a boy, so Blackie is a good name. Oh, dear, he's full of fleas. Take him outside and feed him." She handed Blackie back to her. "I'll make an appointment with an animal doctor, but until he goes to the doctor's office, he has to stay outside."

Amanda carried me back outside with a woebegone look on her face. "You stay here while I get you some food", she said as she put him back down on the porch and went back inside.

I was queasy to my stomach and felt dizzy. "Oh this people thing about being lifted up is a bit too much", I thought as I upchucked. Then I sat down and started to scratch, and scratch. "This dam itch."

Amanda did what she promised for the next two days. Every morning and evening she came out with my two bowls. She sat with me and played with me, chattering on and on about stuff I didn't have an inkling about. In those days I was learning a whole new language and it was tough. I stuck pretty close to the back porch and only wandered off to play with a butterfly or chase a fly. I never ventured back to the barn.

On the third day, Amanda came out without my bowls and her mama came out behind her with a box of some kind. The mama popped it open and said "Okay Blackie, it's time to go to the doctor."

"Uh Oh!" I didn't like the tone of her voice and decided I had better hightail it to safer ground, but her mama was quick. With one motion, she swooped down and picked me up, dumping me into the hole on the top of the box. Even my claws digging into the porch wood didn't help what was happening. Then she closed the top and I was trapped. I yelled for help to Amanda.

Instead of helping me out, she just put her finger through the bars and said, "Its okay little kitten, its okay." That was not reassuring to me in the least and I howled for help over and over.

Now up in the air the cage went and into one of those foul smelling vehicles. Then Amanda and her mama hopped in and we were moving. "Oh, I'm going to die," I whined in fear. I remembered mama's story about the babies that were taken away in the garbage truck and my fear grew and grew. Amanda kept whispering soft words to me, but nothing helped.

Next thing I remembered, I was sitting on a cold table and there was a big man looking down at me, listening to my heart, which was pounding so hard and loudly, I couldn't hear too much of what anyone was saying. Then I was being pushed and prodded, got stuck with something sharp a few times, and then poked in the rectum. "Oh I'm going to die," I kept moaning.

All of a sudden the poking and prodding stopped and the big man picked me up and looked me in the eyes. "What a fine specimen you are Blackie. Your mama did a fine job." Then he held me against his starchy coat and stroked me as he spoke with Amanda and her mama.

"He's a healthy little male kitten. I gave him his shots and took a stool sample for worms. I'll test his blood samples, but I don't expect to find anything. His mama must have been a healthy animal and did a good job with him. He is loaded with fleas though. He's going to need a flea bath. He's a little too young for flea maintenance like "Frontline," but the bath will take care of the problem for now. Leave him with us for a couple of hours, and then he can go home with you."

Amanda was jumping for joy, but I was totally unnerved and sad. Needless to say, when I smelled the horrid shampoo and saw the water, I went ballistic. The assistant to the veterinarian had to give me a shot to calm me down. I fell asleep thinking "so this is what death feels like."

When I woke up, I was back in the box and dizzy. "Am I dead?" I kept thinking, and started to cry.

The vet's assistant felt moved by the little kitten's moaning. She took me out of the box and sat down and cooed to me for a little while. "You'll be going home little boy. You are fine, don't cry." She petted me and kept me in her lap until Amanda came back.

I was tired. Between my office visit, the shots, and my bath, I was exhausted. I didn't argue at all when I went back in my box and into the car.

Once home, Amanda put down my bowls and sat down on the floor with me. "What's the matter little Blackie? It's time to eat dinner," but my stomach was too upset to eat. And I had to go to the bathroom. I knew from my mama that clean cats didn't go anywhere except in the potty corner.

Amanda picked me up and chattered away about sleeping in her room, but first I had to learn where my litter box was. I didn't quite understand what she was talking about as she carried me upstairs to the bathroom and placed me in another box. This one was open and smelled rather sweet. No threat at all.

"This is where you tinkle and poop," Amanda said and sat on the floor and waited.

Blackie started thinking. "What does she want me to do?" I sat in the box and looked at her with a perplexed demeanor. "Humm," I thought. "When mama did this, she was waiting for us to potty. She'd carry us to the potty corner and would sit and wait. Oh well, I'll try it. Can't be any worse then being drowned." So I tinkled, and then instinctively I covered it with the sweet smelling sand.

Amanda was so happy. She jumped up and down saying what a good boy I was and what a clean cat. She yelled to her mama that I knew what a litter box was and cooing at me took me into her bedroom where she put me on her bed. I slept in luxury that night, curled up next to the little girl who made me feel happy and fuzzy inside. "What a wonderful life" I thought as I drifted off to sleep.

Chapter 10

I had another three months of happiness. I was learning English, Amanda was learning a little cat, and I was discovering how strong my mental telepathy capabilities were. What a wonderful life. Even the daddy was nice to me. I had plenty to eat, lots of inside toys, which made Amanda giggle and laugh out loud when I chased them. I learned that Amanda went to school on a bus and I would patiently wait for her return. I would nap and play outside, chase bugs and wander a bit, but was always on the front porch when the school bus dropped her off.

The weather was getting colder by the day outside which made it so nice to have a warm bed and a little girl for warmth to sleep beside. One morning Amanda and I woke up to a white world. We went through our morning ritual of hitting the bathroom and the litter box, down the stairs into the kitchen where Amanda poured my breakfast into my bowl and then to the back door to see what the day would bring.

"Blackie it's snowing," Amanda squealed, as she picked me up off the floor and let me peer out the door window. I had finally gotten use to being picked up, but still, if I was in her arms too long, I started feeling queasy to the stomach. When that feeling started, I would wiggle and squirm to get back down on the ground.

All the color had gone away. In its place was a white blur with dark shadows. "What is going on?" I wondered.

Amanda opened the back door. I did what I do every morning. Charged out the back door. What a surprise. I dashed onto the porch and ran down the stairs. Plop, right into a pile of snow. For a split second, I thought I was stuck and panic set in. I leaped into the air, only to come down in the white stuff again. I repeated this three or four times getting myself turned around and then charged back into the house shaking all that white cold stuff from my fur.

"Ugh, whatever it is stuck to my paws and fur it's cold," I thought as I sat down and started licking and drying my feet.

Amanda broke out into peals of laughter as she watched me. "Silly boy, it's just the first snow of winter. It can't hurt you. It's fun."

"Fun, what fun?" I meowed as I stuck my head out the door and sniffed.

Rushing out the door, Amanda grabbed a handful of the white stuff, came back inside, shut the door and proceeded to make a ball out of it and rolled it towards me.

I backed up rather rapidly as this thing sloshed across the floor. I stretched my nose out to sniff it, whacked it with my paw, then turned around and ran under the kitchen table. While Amanda stood there laughing, I slowly meandered back to the ball, which had started to melt making a little puddle of water. I smelled the water and realizing that was what it was, I tasted it. "Humm," I purred. "Just water. Solid water that turns into liquid in the warm house. What will they think of next?"

Deciding everything was fine, I regained my composure and sauntered off to my bowl to get a bite to eat, watching the white ball with a side glance making sure it didn't follow me.

"Funny, funny cat," Amanda said, as she picked up the remains and dumped it into the sink. Getting some paper towels she dried my back as I ate and wiped the puddle from the floor.

Later in the day, we went outside, and while Amanda played in the snow, I sat on the porch surveying the situation. I did not like this stuff one bit. It was cold and wet and hid the smells of other creatures. There was nothing to chase or stalk. Only a white silence. I'd rather take a nap in the warm house.

One evening, after what the humans called Christmas, Amanda's daddy came home from work in a very serious mood. He and her mama had a very deep conversation in their bedroom. I sensed it was not a good thing whatever it was, and crept into bed with Amanda that night thinking something was devastatingly amiss.

The next day, mama sat Amanda down at the kitchen table. I curled up into her lap and listened to what was going on.

"Daddy has been transferred," her mama said. "We will be moving to another city and we will have to sell this house. The real estate lady is coming today to talk to us about it."

Amanda had all the protests, her friends, her school, her room. The mama had all the answers. New friends, new school, new room. Daddy will be making a lot more money, and that's how the day went.

I sensed her mama didn't seem too happy about the move, but tried very hard to seem like she was happy and comforted Amanda, who was miserable.

For the next few weeks, nothing was the same anymore. Her mama was cleaning and packing. Strangers came and went from the house. In the beginning, I tried to be sociable with the strangers thinking this might make it easier for Amanda and her mama, but some of them didn't like me. One tried to kick me and another kept saying the house smelled like cat, and she couldn't stand the odor.

"Hmmm," I growled back, "I think you stink worse then rat." Then I got spiteful and started jumping up on the kitchen counters or kicking litter out of my box on their feet. Sometimes I would scratch on the furniture or hiss at them. Amanda's Mama would get angry at me and yell. After a while I just went and hid until they left.

I didn't realize it, but I was just mimicking the emotions I was receiving from Amanda. She cried a lot and sometimes got belligerent at her mama. Her momma would yell and banish to her bedroom where she would pout and I would lay in her arms and feel so sad.

Then one day there was the argument that changed my life. They were all in the kitchen when the daddy came home. Since he was being transferred on such short notice, the family did not have time to go house hunting at the new location. His Aunt Betty said that they could stay with her for a while in the interim. In fact she was ecstatic they would be staying with her. There was one major problem. Aunt Betty had severe allergies and one of them was to cats. He told them about this conversation and informed everyone that I could not go with them. The daddy and mama said some harsh words to each other. Amanda was crying and threatening to run away. The mama threw their dinner in the sink and threatened to leave the daddy. Oh, it was a mess that night. I didn't quite understand the meaning of the words, but felt the anger. I did not realize it was my life, as I knew it, that was going to be changed so dramatically, but I sensed a danger. That night Amanda cried herself to sleep hugging me until I thought I was going to be squashed. I didn't move though. For some reason I knew this was going to be the last time I was going to be here and I cried myself to sleep with her.

The next morning while I was eating breakfast, the daddy picked me up and put me in the cat carrier. That was the last I ever saw of my warm house, my bowl and Amanda. My life as a kitten had ended.

PART III

Adolescence

Chapter 11

The daddy took the cat carrier out to the car and we drove for what seemed like a long time. Then the daddy carried me into a building that reeked of other animals. There, at the desk, the daddy wrote out a check for my care and food for one month and donated the cat carrier to the animal shelter. The woman at the desk promised him that they would find a good home for me during that time.

After the daddy left, the woman picked up the cat carrier and brought me into another room. It was a long corridor with cages on both sides with big dogs, little dogs and puppies stinking of a strong chemical, which to me, didn't mask the smell of urine and stale blood.

Through that room she marched, opened another door, into another long corridor smelling of the same strong chemical. Here the cages were much smaller in double rows on both sides. I smelled the overwhelming stink of cat urine and feces. It made me sick and if I hadn't been so frightened, I would have barfed all over myself. My eyes grew big as I watched cage after cage of other cats pass by, all with the same haunted hungry look in their eyes. The woman finally stopped, picked up the carrier, opened the door and shook me out into one of those cages. Then she slammed the cage door shut, and I heard the bolt slam shut.

I was in an upper cage. The cages were quite small, maybe three feet by three feet and bars on all four sides with no floor. Under the cage was newspaper, stretched out as far as I could see. My paper was clean, but others had urine and feces laying on it. The bars under my feet were putting odd pressure on my paws and it was uncomfortable to stand in one position.

Looking down the line of cages, I saw cats and more cats of various size and color. The smaller cats, like me, still just kittens, had room to move around. The full-grown cats had barely enough room to change position let alone stand up for any length of time. Each cell had two bowls, one of water and the other of food.

I lay down to ease the discomfort on my paws and started licking them. "What is going to happen to me? Why am I here? What did I do to be sent here?" I whined all these questions half aloud.

"Stupid little runt," the cat to my right growled. "This is where they put you because the humans don't want us around anymore. If we do not find another home, they put us to sleep forever. You're a little squirt, so someone will probably come and take you home. Me, I'm an old fat Tom and no one will want me. I'm going to die all because my owner never cleaned my litter box, so I peed on the floor just one too many times."

Just when I was going to ask a question, I heard the cat on my left purr, "Is that my little squeaky son?"

I spun around, and sure enough, it was mama in the cage next to me. I crawled over to the bars separating us and rubbed against them catching the warmth and smell of my mama between the metal. I laid my head down and cried, "Why are you here mama?"

"Oh my son, I don't know what happened to me. I have been very tired carrying this new litter. When it was my time to give birth, I wasn't as cautious as I should have been in picking out my nest and the humans caught us. We were dumped into a bag and carried here. My new babies are not well either. I lost two at birth and these two are not doing well at all. I think my Tom gave me something very bad."

"Your new babies?"

"Yes my son." She moved her body ever so slightly and exposed the two little kittens that were nursing on her teats. "I am not producing milk the way I should, and these poor babies are not getting enough to eat."

"Mama, you can't be sick. You have so much life to give and so many more babies to teach."

"What happened to your humans?"

"They are moving to a big city and can't take me with them. Amanda cried for two days and said she was going to run away and find me. Do you think she'll be able to find me here?"

"Humph," mama growled. "Just like all humans. I warned you. They cannot be trusted. She will not come for you. She is a child and children have to stay with their parents until they are old enough to go out on their own, just like us, only much longer."

I mewled a bit knowing what mama said was the truth. I just didn't want to accept the fact that I was stuck here in a cage.

Then I thought of my sisters. "Are they here too mama?"

"No my squeaky one. They found homes like you and as far as I know, they are still there. After you left, they started thinking about the life you were leading. They would sneak out and lay in the bushes watching you and waiting to see what would happen. You looked so happy to them that they decided to try for homes with humans. They became more friendly and playful with the neighbors of your Amanda and wound up living with them. It was time for your sisters to move on anyway. My baby cycle was coming and my Tom was calling me. It was all for the better anyway, because my Tom would have taken them too and they would be sick like me."

"Mama, you can't be sick. It's not fair. Please don't be sick," I yowled loud and long.

Mama just smiled and told me that she had a good life and just raising prize kittens like me and my sisters were well worth the life she lived. "One more thing I want you to do. I want you to escape from here as soon as you can and by any means that you can. There are other cats here as ill as I am, and others just plain mean and nasty. They would hurt you given the chance. I want you out of here as soon as you get the chance to go, and if that means being nice to humans, do it. Escape from here somehow, some way. Promise me now," she mewed and then groaned in pain as she laid her head down.

"I promise you I'll escape mama, I promise."

I realized she had fallen asleep and did look very tired. The poor kittens were mewling in hunger at her belly and suddenly I knew they were going to die. I knew too that my mama was going to leave this earth and it made me so sad. "I'll make it mama," I cried, determined beyond any emotion I had felt before.

I fitfully slept for a short while, dreaming of Amanda, the warm kitchen and my soft bed. I woke up to a thunderous clunk of the cages and watched as a man with a stick and a hose walked down the aisle of cages. One by one, he opened them and squirted water into the bowls with the stick at ready. Only once did he use it when a big old cat lunged out the open door. Whonk, right on top of the cat's head and I heard an awful howl of pain erupt from the cat, then silence. Escape didn't mean getting hurt like that, it meant using your brain, so I cowered in the back of my cell while the man filled my water bowl, watching. When the man got to mama's cage, he stopped what he was doing, put down the stick and hose, opened the cage, prodded mama with his hand and then talked into a box he was carrying in his shirt pocket. The woman who had carried me in and dumped me in my cage came running.

My mama had gone to sleep never to wake up again. The woman, carrying a sack, put my mama into it. Then the man picked up the kittens and one at a time snapped their necks and put them in there with her. I was so shocked by this that I sat motionless for what seemed an eternity. When I got back my senses, the man had finished filling the rest of the water bowls and was leaving. The woman had vanished with my mama and half siblings.

I howled a rage and loss that was deep and uncontrollable. My tail shot up and I sprayed every corner, every bar of the cage. My hair was standing up all over my body like a Halloween cat as I howled and sprayed. I looked like a kitten gone insane and for one inconsolable instant of my life, I wanted to kill the evil man and woman. I hated humans and wanted vengeance. I paced my confinement until my paws bled, and still I paced.

Hours later and in pain, I finally lay down. Sobbing now, I licked the blood from my paws and fell asleep. I woke up very hungry and thirsty, so I tried out the water and food. The water was okay, but the food tasted like sawdust. Then I laid down again mostly because my paws were so sore and thought about how I was going to escape from this prison.

I thought maybe I could open the lock, so I started picking at with my claws and teeth.

"What are you doing numb nuts?" the big cat next door asked.

"Trying to open the lock and get out of here bully," I responded.

"Ain't gonna work. You'll ruin your teeth and break your claws stupid. There is no way out."

I sighed and laid down. "The bully was right. This wasn't the way to do it."

Chapter 12

For two days, I laid there, drinking water but not eating. I was losing weight and my shiny black coat was getting dull and matted. I didn't clean myself except to try to heal my paws, and I wouldn't talk to any of the other cats. On the third morning something different happened. The evil man pulled all the old stinky newspaper out, replacing it with clean paper. Then all the water bowls were filled and fresh food placed in the dishes.

Talking aloud to all the cats, he said. "Visiting day. People are coming. Maybe one of you rats will find a home."

"Spruce up," the bully said to me, "maybe this will be your lucky day. People like you little guys. This could be your chance to get out of here."

I looked at him and didn't even respond. "I've had enough humans for the rest of my life," I thought.

Well, the humans arrived, looking in one cage after another. All of my fellow prisoners perked up, doing dances, licking fingers, meowing coyly, puffing their fur. Not me. "I'm not a puppet on a stage. I don't want human companions. I want out of here and away from them forever."

A young woman and man passed by my cage two or three times murmuring to each other. "He looks so sad and little, and so serious for a kitten." Finally, they decided to have a better look at me and asked the evil man to open the cage. The young woman picked me up and started to stroke me softly, as Amanda did. I wanted so desperately to respond to the kind touch, but I was too angry and too saddened by what had happened in such a short time. She put me down on the floor and at the same time, the door to the room opened.

I saw a chance of escape and charged past a new human coming in and out into the room full of dogs. There were humans there also, talking to the dogs and each other. The dogs spotted me. Suddenly there was a cacophony of yowling, barking, and sharp teeth snapping at the bars. I skidded to a stop, changed direction, screeched to a halt, and bolted in a different direction. The humans got upset and I could sense the fear of the dogs in them. The evil man bounded through the door from the cat room at the same time the vile woman opened the door to the office. I spotted my opening, with one mad leap, I flung myself at the woman's feet, and slid through the opening just as the door swung shut. The main door to the outside was opening and without even gaining balance, I hurled myself outside, rolled down the two steps, gained footing and fled as if the devil was chasing me. I didn't even stop at the tree line, but ran across the parking lot into the woods. I ran for as long and as fast as I was able, until I was breathless. I stopped then and yowled at the woods, "I'm free mama, I'm free."

Chapter 13

Oh, I was tired. Lack of decent food, sore paws and thirsty, I realized I was free, but definitely not out of danger. It was cold outside and there was a combination of snow and ice covering the ground. I smelled the air. It still had a chill to it, but it also had another smell. Even though the tree trunks were still gray and the bushes bare, the air had the yearning smell of green grass and blossoming flowers.

I lay still, drifting in and out of sleep for a while on a bed of leaves, my ears unconsciously listening for anything that sounded different then the normal noises. Coming back out of my fugue, I listened more intently to a noise that maybe promised something.

It was a distant gurgling, like the sound of water running from the faucet of the house. I got up and limped my way towards the sound. As I followed the noise, it became louder and more of a rushing until I suddenly got the whiff of definite water. I was moving faster now angling down hill towards the sound when I did something very un-cat like. I slipped and rolled downhill almost into a small creek of water. Plopped right down on some very cold stones. Shaking my head and gaining my footing, I sniffed at the water, and then tasted it. It was heaven. So cold, it was numbed my tongue, but I drank until my thirst was quenched.

Then I sat up, stretched and surveyed the area. I was at the bottom of a very high hill forested with many trees. The creek wasn't very wide where I landed, and the water was still. The rushing noise was higher up the mountain as a small waterfall cascaded down into the creek. Across the creek, the woods were on level ground as far as I could see.

Movement on the other side of the creek caught my attention and I flattened myself against the cold stones and became motionless except for my whiskers, which were feeling the vibrations for information. Out of the woods walked a very big creature, with large ears and a fluffy white tail that looked like a soft cotton ball ... With her were two smaller ones. They looked just like the large animal except for coloring. The big one was brown in color whereas the little ones were brown with white speckles. "They must be babies," I watched in dead stealth, except for my tail, which decided to twitch, while they all went to the edge of the creek and started to drink.

One of the babies caught the movement of my tail and looked up. She stared at me for a while and then said, "Hello cat." I spooked and backed away, which immediately caught the attention of the adult and all three darted away from the creek, stopping at the fringes of the woods looking around. I sat up and thought, "Damn tail. Why does it act up when I least want it too?"

The baby who had spoke to me took two steps forward and said, "What are you doing way out here?"

My eyes got wide, and the words just toppled out. "I escaped from prison and I am a free cat. My mama made me promise to become free. Who are you?"

"You mean feral cat, don't you?" snorted the adult deer. "Let's go children. Ferals can be dangerous."

"Wait mama, he's not feral. He doesn't smell mean."

"What is feral?" I asked.

"Feral means a cat with no home. A cat that never lived with humans, although my dad says all cats are feral and dangerous," replied the fawn.

"Humans are dangerous", snapped the mother.

"I lived with humans once," I said. "The daddy said I couldn't go with them and he took me to prison. My mama died there, but before she went, she made me promise to be free, and I am. Your mother is right about humans. They are mean." With that, I lay down, put my head on my paws and mewled my sadness. "I miss Amanda, warm bed and food bowls so badly."

"Don't cry little cat", said the fawn. "There is plenty of food and shelter in these woods for you. You just have to look."

"What are you called?" I asked .

"We are deer," replied the little one, and this is our mother ..." With that, they all turned in unison and trotted off into the darkness of the trees.

I sat for moment thinking about what had just happened. I realized that they had not really spoken aloud. It was more of a body language, mind touching type of thing. I understood what they said, and as they did me.

"Umm, it was like Amanda and me. It was totally intriguing and exciting. I realized I could communicate with so many. In addition, it then saddened me because I had no one to talk with. I was all alone again. I picked myself up, stretched and wandered across the creek heading into the woods in which the deer had disappeared.

I crossed the creek. The water was shallow, no higher than my hindquarter, but bitter cold. I hardly felt it. I was feeling a combination of excitement about the future, the happiness of being free, fear of the unknown and exhaustion.

Chapter 14

Once across the stream, I realized it would be dark soon. The forest was full of shadows, the air was getting colder and my feet were just about numb from the water crossing. I had to find shelter for the night. Investigating my surroundings, I noticed several spruce and pine trees in the area. I knew pine trees gave more protection from the wind and cold than the other trees. The low branches and needles under these trees helped retain the warmth of the day better then leaves. The fragrance of the pine would help mask my smell and keep me safe. I didn't understand how I knew all of this, but I did.

Shortly, I found a tree of my liking. The lower branches were heavy and laying low to the ground forming a cave-like atmosphere. Sliding in under them, I crawled to the south side of the tree, dug a bit in the needles until they were to my liking, circled around a few times, then curled up and went instantly to sleep.

Cats in the wild are normally nocturnal creatures, being the most active in the wee hours of the morning. Because I was so tired, I slept the whole night through. not coming fully awake until the sun was up. It was dangerous for me to sleep so sound, but nature was protecting me.

What I did not know was my ancient ancestors and those after had embedded in my genetic coding vast amounts of information. While I slept, my ears listened to the sounds of the night in the forest and the fur on my back absorbed tons of information into my brain. I would always know the difference between normal and something out of the ordinary. Something different and my body would become fully alert and ready to flee or fight almost immediately.

Upon awakening, I was famished. I stretched, stood up and peeked out of my cave with whiskers twitching, ears alert. I sensed a light vibration on the ground and turned my keen eyesight in that direction. Scurrying across some oak leaves about twenty feet away was a field mouse carrying an acorn. I crouched down, hindquarter ready to spring. The only movement I made was my whiskers determining the distance of pounce.

An odd sound was coming out of my throat, which mesmerized the mouse. It stopped its scurrying and it sat up and looked directly into my eyes. In a split second, maybe a blink of an eye, I flew through the air and landed on my breakfast.

Chapter 15

My life went like this for the next couple of weeks. The world, as I knew it, was heading into early spring and it started to warm up slightly during the day, but the evenings brought a cooling down and night brought below freezing temperatures. I explored my environment, but never strayed too far from my den. Knowing, in order to survive, that I must stay warm during the night. I was lonely too. I hadn't seen the deer since our encounter and the only other animals I did see were my meals. As I prowled the forest around my den, I sprayed the trees, marking my territory.

One day, in the third week of my exile, the weather started to turn bitter again. The wind started to howl making the trees wail and the sky grayed deeply, making noon seem like dusk. I knew that some foul weather was coming. The air smelled like snow and I did not like snow one bit. This made me think of Amanda and the ball of snow in the kitchen. How she loved the snow, I thought and in turn, this made me remember my warm bed in the house. I realized, this was the first time in a long time that I thought of my past life, and it saddened me. I shrugged it off and made my way back to my den.

It snowed for a day and a half. One of the worst late March snow storms in upstate New York history. The branches of the pine tree were laden with snow, making my den look like an igloo of sorts. I was warm, but hungry and very lonely, sleeping a lot for those two days. When the weather cleared, I plowed my way out from under the branches into the cold white world. The snow was quite deep and I had a heck of a time walking in it. Working my way down to the stream, I finally drank, lapping up the cold water, much more thirsty than I thought I would be.

The world seemed very silent in the snow and nothing was moving, except for the trees, which swayed with the wind. "Damn," I thought, "now I have to find something to eat."

Out of the corner of my eye, I caught movement under the water of the stream. Turning around, I crouched down and watched a silvery streak flitting around the rocks. I watched it for quite some time, noting the patterns of movement it made. The water was bitter cold, but I couldn't stop the desire to catch whatever it was. I batted at it with my paws and the first couple of tries were a miss, the third a near miss. I crouched down again, and when I felt the time was right, I pounced, whole body into the water, teeth bared and claws fully extended. I felt my claws sink into soft flesh and in one motion, I flung the fish as far as I could into the bank, came out of the water, pounced and bit down. I had gotten myself a very large rainbow trout. I stuffed myself on fish and decided it was as good as snake.

"There is so much still left over," I thought. "If I leave it, something else might get my dinner." I dragged it between my legs through the deep snow until I reached my den. Pulling it under the branches with me, I felt so satisfied, and napped knowing I had dinner that night. I didn't know that what I had done left a trail to my hiding place for others to find.

As night approached, I heard some very different sounds. They were the howling of another animal, and sounded very dangerous. I heard several others answer, and it put a chill up my spine. I stayed very quiet and listened. Whatever it was, it was fairly close. Then I caught the smell of what was out there. It had the dark evil smell, like a rat, only much larger. Probing with my mind, I felt a chill. The mind, I sensed, was dark and brooding, looking for food. It hit me like a slap in the face. This animal was looking for me. It was outside my den and it knew I was in here. Slinking silently to the north side of the tree, I didn't know what I was going to do. My heart was beating so fast and so loud, I was sure it was going to pop out of my chest. With this thought in my mind, the animal outside uttered a low intense growl and attacked the spot where I had been laying, spraying pine needles, snow and spittle all over my warm little den. I fled, running as fast as my legs could move, leaping through the snow. The coyote spotted me and tore through the branches on the other side of the tree snapping his jaws at my hind legs. The stench of its breath was an overwhelming odor to me and I knew I was doomed. In a split second, I was going to be dinner for another animal, and then, I thought, climb. Climb as fast as I can.

I leaped at a nearby oak tree with back and front claws fully extended and climbed. About thirty feet up, I thought my hind legs were going to give out, so I reached for a branch and hauled my body onto it. I looked down and saw the animal jumping at the tree, trying to claw its way up. Out of frustration, the animal howled as loud as he could muster, "I am coyote, and you are my dinner, cat. I will catch you." Then the forest came alive with similar howls, "catch it, eat it, catch it." I crouched low to the branch and shivered in my terror.

The coyote stayed under the tree all night. First, he howled in anger, and then whined in frustration, all the while clawing at the tree, always looking up at me staring right into my eyes. As daylight approached, the howling became deafening, coming from all parts of the forest, and then suddenly it got very quiet. The coyote looked me one more time in the eyes and growled, "I will be back for you. You will be my next meal." Then he sullenly wandered away.

I was terrified and my body felt shocky. I could not gain the strength to move, so I shut my eyes and took some deep breaths. I wondered if I had even breathed the whole time I was up there. I started to cry, little meows that sounded so forlorn. I didn't know how long I had stayed in that state of mind, but after a while, I realized my muscles were aching so badly that I would have to move. When I stood up, the branch swayed, and I thought I was going to fall, so I latched on with my claws for dear life.

Backing myself up, my butt hit the tree trunk. Straddling the branch, I slowly hooked my back claws on to the trunk of the tree, swung my body over and dug in with my front claws, then backed myself down about fifteen feet and lost my footing.

Balancing my body in the fall, I managed to land on all fours, the snow absorbing some of the shock. Testing my legs, I realized I was fine, but every muscle in my body ached. I walked back to my den and discovered that I still had some of my fish. The smell of the coyote was everywhere and it triggered the fear again. I knew I couldn't stay here anymore. I dragged the remains of the fish into the open where the stench wasn't so bad, ate, and then wandered down to the creek where I drank some water. Then I turned my back on what had become another lost home and wandered away through the snow, following the creek down stream.

# Chapter 16

For the next few days, I slept only during the day, burrowing down between rocks and snow, staying close to the stream. I would travel at night, always on the alert for any sounds or smells that were unusual. Food was scarce. Only twice in those several days was I able to catch myself a mouse. I gorged myself on it, and became violently ill, vomiting up my whole meal. I had eaten too fast, and my stomach had shrunk from lack of food. I buried it to hide any smells that would attract an enemy. The second go round, although famished, I only ate half, then thought that this was as good a place as any to rest.

The sun was coming up and my body was really starting to feel the stress. my muscles hurt, and I felt like an old man at seven months. I found a comfortable spot between rocks, and knew they would warm up in the sun. I placed the half-eaten mouse nearby, dug away the snow from the rocks, went round and round positioning myself, found a comfortable spot and lay down. With some protein in my body, I began to relax, and without meaning to, I fell into a deep sleep. Something I hadn't done in what seemed like forever.

When I woke up, the sun was getting low in the western sky. It was time to move on, but first, I finished eating the mouse, stretched, took a long deep lap of water, cleaned myself thoroughly, and then, started trudging on.

About two miles into my journey, I sensed movement, and watched the shadows intensely. In one of the shadows, low to the ground, under a maple tree was an animal. My whiskers caught the vibration of something slightly larger then me, very slow and lumbersome in movement. "Hummm, I wonder if it would be something good to eat," I thought, as I inched myself closer to the maple tree. I finally caught a whiff of it on a pre-evening gust of wind. It was nothing I had smelled before. A gamey, heavy smell, but definitely not an evil, foul odor.

Inching closer and closer, I suddenly had the daylights scared out of me.

"Ach," screamed the strange creature. It turned its head into the tree and began yelling, "Don't hurt me, don't hurt me," as needles flew off its body helter skelter in my direction. They flew all over the forest floor, up in the air like missiles, one striking a nearby tree and penetrating it. I was lucky I had crouched low to the ground, and none of the spines hit me directly.

"Stop it," yowled Blackie.

"Go away," screamed the porcupine.

"Okay, Okay, but quit it will you?"

"You'd eat me if you had the chance and I won't give you that chance," snarled the animal.

"I'm not a coyote," growled Blackie. "I'm just a cat and not big enough to catch you to eat."

The creature turned his head away from the tree and looked at me, seeing a cat of small stature, not much more then a kitten. "I'm foraging for dinner and you scared me. What would you expect a porcupine to do?" sniffled the animal. "If you were bigger, you would have tried to have me for dinner."

"Maybe, but you're too big and ornery and probably tough like shoe leather. I'm just working myself back to civilization. I've had enough forest. I'm tired and hungry. Was chased by coyotes. I'm going to become a feral cat and live in the city where I was born. At least there is enough food and places to sleep that are safe. Humans aren't half as dangerous as the creatures in this place. At least you know what to expect from them."

"Humans? Woe is I little cat. I'd rather be here then live with them. They smell bad and are much more dangerous then what dwells here. However, if you are looking for them, they live a few miles from here. Just down at the bottom of this creek, there is a great road where cars drive by very fast. Killed my mate this winter. Mowed him over. Poof, just like that. There are houses along the road and I hear cities on both ends of it. Now go away and let me find my dinner or I'll let fly my spines again and maybe this time I'll hit you." With that, the porcupine waddled off, foraging under the leaves and snow.

"What a place," I thought as I roamed off, again following the stream. "At least I have more information then I did before."

Chapter 17

A bit further, down the stream, the terrain started to change. I wandered into open fields surrounded by fencing and saw a large barn in the distance to my west. "Could be shelter for the night," I thought, and loped off heading for the barn. I felt a sharp pain in my right front paw, and had to stop and sit to examine it. Little balls of ice were forming between the already damaged pads on the bottom of my paws. Apparently, one of the globs of ice penetrated the sensitive flesh between the pads, and I was bleeding, the white ice turning pink in the fading sunlight. I took a great sigh, and proceeded to clean the ice particles from out between the pads, but not before surveying the landscape and sniffing for danger. Took me quite a while to clean them thoroughly and the sun was starting to sink into the horizon quickly. Standing up I now noticed I had ice lumps hanging off my tail. "I'm a mess," I growled, as I limped off towards the barn.

The barn doors were shut and bolted, but surveying the building, I found a broken board with a space wide enough for me to squeeze through. Once inside, I smelled the sweet pungent odor of mowed hay, and my eyes adjusted to the gloom. There was another smell, an animal smell even stronger then the hay.

Moving slowly, making no noise, I inched my way through the shadows towards the back of the barn where the smell was the greatest. There, in a stall, was a huge animal chewing on hay. Lying next to her was another large animal, identical except that it was much smaller in comparison and sleeping. The smell of these animals was definitely not dangerous to me. I knew, although I did not know how I knew. Mesmerized by their size and demeanor, I jumped up on the stall wall and stared into a pair of huge, sad and dewy eyes.

"Hello barn cat," the animal said.

I mewled, "What are you?"

"I'm a belted Galloway breeder cow and this is my heifer baby," as she moved her head in the direction of the calf.

"How do you know I'm a cat?"

"Humans keep you guys around all the time to help keep the vermin population down. Helps to keep us healthy. Was a big male Tom use to live with us for a long time. He went away not too long ago and never came back. Are you going to stay awhile?"

"Definitely for the night. I need to sleep and let my paws heal."

"Enjoy your stay then," the cow said, as she bent down to retrieve some more hay.

I jumped down from the stall wall and started to explore. It was a two-story barn with bales of hay stacked everywhere. I climbed the stairs to the second floor and smiled. "The perfect place to sleep tonight."

I roamed around and found a half broken bale somewhere in the center of the hay maze. Squirreling myself down into it, I could feel the warmth of the grasses.

Between the smell of the hay and cattle, I knew my odor was well masked. Purring with contentment, I drifted off into a deep sleep.

I slept for three days. I hadn't realized how desperate a condition my body was in. Pain loomed everywhere inside of me and my feet hurt terribly. Every muscle in my young body rebelled when I walked or jumped, but survival was of utmost importance. Without safety, I knew I was doomed. So, I plodded along for what had seemed forever. My learning mind had shut down and I was moving on genetic knowledge. Knowledge, which was passed down generation after generation. The things I "just knew" were part of this network of knowledge I was born with, along with my super strong desire to survive. Now, that I felt safe in the loft, my body relaxed and started to heal. I'd come out of my sleep into a semi-conscious state, lick my frostbitten paws, drift back to sleep, come back to the surface and clean my body, and sleep again. My subconscious took over and my whiskers, the hair on my body and sense of smell stayed semi-alert, checking the environment for me while I slept, making sure all was normal.

The owner of the farm had come and gone on a daily basis, taking hay to feed his animals, but my subconscious didn't see any danger, so it let me sleep. Finally, on the fourth day, thirst and hunger drove me fully awake. I was achy, parched and famished. Far from the healthy kitten I had been such a short while ago, my body was very thin, my shiny coat was dull and I felt very weak.

I stretched, my head felt fuzzy and I became a little dizzy. I needed food and drink desperately. I stretched again, listened to my environment, heard nothing different, went down the barn stairs and squeezed out the opening I had come through.

It was a gray daylight and warmer then a few days ago. The snow was starting to melt. Icicles, dripping water, were hanging from the barn eves. I had been prepared to eat the snow, but when I saw the puddles, I smiled, walked over to one and drank to my heart's content. The water was cold, but felt sublime on my dry tongue and parched throat. My body responded to the fluids too, and my dizziness and some of the weakness dissipated. My stomach started to growl fiercely, and I knew I had to get some food and soon. I looked around and listened. There didn't seem to be anything moving outside. Early spring brought wet and gray weather, so smaller animals were in their borrows or hiding out in warm buildings.

I squeezed myself back through the board into the barn, thinking maybe I'd find a mouse and listened. At first, I didn't pick up the phishing sound, but as I ambled around the lower level of the barn, it became more audible to me. I crouched, whiskers and ears alert, listening and feeling for the vibrations that would give the location of whatever it was. It sounded like it was coming from inside one of the walls of the barn. Slinking closer, I listened intently. The noise sounded so familiar to me. I was sure it wasn't a mouse, but something else I'd heard before. Then it dawned on me. It was when I was a kitten playing in the grass where mama had told me not to go. My first kill, snake. I started to drool, the saliva dripping from my mouth. If anyone had seen me, they would have thought me mad with distemper, but I was so hungry my body responded to just the thought of food.

Quiet and still, I strained all my senses in the direction of the phishing noise. It wasn't in the wall; it was just beneath a pile of debris next to the wall. Inching closer and closer, I noticed there was a subtlety to the noise. The snake wasn't moving normally. It was more of a straining, wiggling in one spot more so than a forward movement. Then I caught the motion with my keen sight. It was a snake. A very large one and it was doing something that startled me. It was crawling out of its skin. Just knowing, I realized the snake was molting and was very vulnerable at this moment. Without hesitation, I sprung forward and down on the snake. With one deft blow of my front claws, I hit the snake behind its head, sinking claws deep into flesh. Then I bit down with my teeth in a crushing blow. The snake slithered violently, rolling me on my side and then my back, but I held on, biting harder and deeper into its head and eyes. The snake with one last roll, slipped silently into stillness. I let go, regained my footing and stared down at my catch. It was huge. At least four times my length or more. A normal cat wouldn't attempt a kill of such a large snake because of the danger to itself, but I was a desperately hungry cat. This was all or nothing survival.

It was a rat snake, common to most barns, and a large one at that. It lived on small rodents and was healthy and good for farmers and their cattle. To me it was great food. I had to rest before I could even take my first bite, so I lay down next to the snake and caught my wind. I didn't know that I was in an extremely weakened state. If I had not made the kill this first time, I most likely would not have had the strength to try again and would have starved to death. I bit into the flesh and swallowed some nourishment. Remembering how ill I had gotten by gorging myself on the mouse, I ate slowly and not too much. Then I cleaned myself and started to think of how I would get my catch up the stairs to the second floor of the barn. I tried dragging it a distance, but it was too heavy for me to get very far, let alone get it up the stairs. Finally I dragged it back to the debris where I caught it, ate a little bit more, and then covered it as best I could. Then I climbed back upstairs to my bed, made myself comfortable with a few turns and went back to sleep.

Chapter 18

I now had shelter, plenty of water and food for several days. I rested most of the time, healing, and cleaning myself until my hair started to shine again. My body started to gain back a little weight and I started to feel stronger. The pain in my feet lessened more every day. Most of my excursions were in the nighttime when the barn was still and quiet. During the day, workers and the farmer would come and go with large machinery, making all kinds of noises. They even laughed occasionally which made me remember Amanda and her giggles.

My snake was all gone and I had to start thinking about food again. One early morning, I had caught myself a mouse and was sitting out in the open on the second floor of the barn, contemplating my catch, when the farmer entered the barn. My first instinct was to run, so I scurried behind a bale of hay and listened. The farmer went about his business down below, acting as if he had not seen me. "Whew, what a close call. I've got to be more careful until I decide to leave."

The farmer went back to the house, took off his boots, hung his jacket and hat on the pegs in the mudroom and went in to have breakfast and spoke to his wife. "Mary, we have a new barn cat. Saw him this morning. I knew he was there, after I found a snake carcass, but hadn't seen him before. Good hunter taking down a snake that size."

How exciting Harry. It was sad when we put Chico down. Worse when the kittens and mama cat had to be killed."

"Yeah, I was attached to that Tom. Ornery as a cat can be, but a good mouser. He was a good boy, but we can't have FIV virus out there with the breeders. Anyway, this is a young male and quite the handsome boy. Black as the Ace of spades with a white patch on his chest that looks like a bow tie. Looks like he's dressed to the nines in a tuxedo."

"I'll have to bring some food and water out to the barn for him. Let him get used to us," Mary said.

"Yep, he'll be a good barn cat. But remember, we'll still have to have him tested and if he's positive, we get rid of him before you get attached."

Later that morning, Mary went out with a bowl of dry cat food, filled another bowl with fresh water and left them near the debris where the snake had been. I watched and wondered. I didn't go near it all day. Distrust of humans was now part of my nature. Late that night, when all was still, I sneaked up on the two bowls half expecting something terrible to happen. I watched them for a while. I batted the food bowl with my paw and then ran a distance. Nothing happened. I inched closer again smelling the luscious aroma of food. It became too much for me to deal with. Nothing was happening, so if the humans want to feed me, fine. With that thought, I indulged in a good wholesome meal. This food did not taste like sawdust at all. More like what Amanda had fed me.

Next day, Mary re-filled the bowls and left. At night, I would eat. This went on for three days.

On the fourth morning, I waited for her on the stairs leading to the second floor.

"Good morning young man. You are a handsome cat, just as Harry said. Are you hungry?"

"Of course I'm hungry," I snapped, "Now go away and let me eat."

However, the human didn't go away. Instead, she stood up, backed away from the bowls, put her hands on her hips and said. "Well little guy, if you want a meal, you are going to have to put up with me being around. Harry said you are a good hunter. I don't want you eating those rodents. We just want you to keep them out of our barn."

I pondered a bit, knowing she was a decent human. "I can't trust humans anymore, but if she wants to feed me just because I can hunt my own meals, why not?" With this thought, I stood up, stretched, meandered down the stairs and over to the bowl, and proceeded to eat.

"Oh my, what a precious kitty you are," Mary said as she bent over and petted my back.

I turned and looked at her with as much disdain as I could muster, swished my tail a bit and then went back to eating.

Mary smiled. "My oh my, are you the independent and handsome one. Dressed to the nines as if you're ready to cat about town."

For a short while, I was known as Mr. Cat About, or Cat for short.

Chapter 19

It was a bit of a shock to me those first few weeks. Mary would come out to the barn several times a day to talk with me. The farmer was a little aloof at first and would keep reminding her not to be too attached to the animal until he was checked by the Vet.

Then, one day the Vet showed up. Mary came out in the morning, but instead of just petting me and talking to me, she plopped me in a cage, carried me back to the house and left me in the cat carrier in the kitchen. I noticed the dog in the yard, but was beside myself with fear remembering the cat prison, unsure of why these nice people would be doing this to me. I cried for help repeatedly, and no one paid any attention except to say it would be all right.

What an ordeal. The Vet prodded and poked. Then she came at me with a giant needle and took blood. I remembered my visit to the doctor when just a kitten. Humph, I mewled. "At least she won't kill me, but why oh why do they have to prod and poke and then prick you with those spines of theirs?"

"Want me to give him his shots today Harry?" the vet asked. "He's quite healthy and handsome at that," as she stuck me with the needle.

"I'd like to do that, but I want to make sure he's FIV negative before I spend more money on the little guy."

I kept thinking to myself "What are they talking about? Just let me be. I'll leave if you don't want me here. Don't you understand that, I'm not a FIV, I'm a cat."

Harry worried for nothing. My blood test came back fine. "I told you I was a cat and not an FIV!"

I had to suffer another day of needles for various diseases, surviving the humiliation, but not without protest. I managed to get in a few swipes of the claws and was able to draw some blood from the doctor, which gave me a great feeling of satisfaction, especially when I realized I could hurt back.

After the doctor visits, my life became one of routine, which I loved. My job was a simple and enjoyable one. Catch the mice and other small rodents that entered the barn.

I was an excellent hunter, so this was just a piece of cake for me. Mary was just a lovely human that fed me well. I liked the farmer too, but did not trust him, so I kept my distance.

I was so well fed; I had no need to eat the mice anymore so I played with them instead. Sometimes, when I was bored, I would stalk a mouse, catch it, let it go, watch it flop around or run, catch it again. I would do this for an hour or so just honing my skills and playing my game. Eventually I would strike, kill, and go off to groom myself and take a nap.

The farmer would come into the barn in the morning with a shovel and wander around checking for dead vermin. When he found one of my kills, he would pick it up with the shovel and dispose of it in a bag, saying, "You're such a good boy and a great hunter, but too bad I can't teach you to dispose of these critters."

I would follow at a distance and watch him scoop up my treasures and listening to the farmer's thoughts and wondering if the farmer ate the mice.

"I don't like the way they smell after a few days anyway, so maybe I'll bring them to him."

Chapter 20

The weather was getting nicer. Spring had popped its bounty. Multicolored flowers bloomed along with the dogwood and cherry trees. I figured it was time to introduce myself to the dog and see what would happen. Off to the yard I went, jumped up on the fence and waited.

I didn't like dogs in particular. I knew some were friendly, but most would chase a cat until the cat tired and had to turn and fight. Nine times out of ten, a dog would back down from our ferocious teeth and pain inducing claws. Sometimes though, a dog would get the better of a cat, usually an older one or a kitten and woe to that cat. The dog would pick it up and fling it or shake it maybe to death or even worse, break its back. I don't know how I knew this, but I did, so I was quite leery of strange dogs and avoided them as much as possible.

This one had a different smell than the dogs in the streets when I was a kitten and a much better odor then the acrid smell of the prison dogs. I hopped up on the fence and looked down. The dog was lying down by the back door steps. He was a full-grown German shepherd with dark markings. Ferocious looking, but I didn't smell danger. The dog noticed me, got up and wandered over to the fence in an amicable manner.

The dog looked up at me and said, "hello cat" quite loudly with a deep resounding bark.

I almost took off, but then I thought, "Why should I do that? I'm safe from him up here and all he said was hello. Puffing myself up and getting ready to respond, the dog suddenly stood up against the fence, put his face in mine and barked, "I said hello."

Startled, I arched my back and every hair on my body stood at attention. "Don't try and scare me you ugly mongrel," I snapped back, and slapped the dog across the nose with my paw, claws extended.

The dog dropped down on all fours and yelped in pain, "What did you do that for?"

"Boys, boys, knock it," off Mary yelled, as she came out the door. "Don't you guys know its okay to get along?"

The dog ran over to her, wagging his tail and hugged up against her waiting to be petted. I figured, I could do one better, stretched my body, sat down, and meowed my interest.

She immediately came over to me, picked me up off the fence, cuddled me in her arms and said to the dog, "Thor, this is our new family member. He is our new barn cat. You must be nice to him."

Thor barked his protest. "I didn't do anything to him mistress. He swiped me with his claws and hurt my nose."

"Now, now Thor, be a good boy," Mary said to the dog, as she reached down with one hand to pet him. Then she noticed his nose was bleeding. Using both hands, Mary picked me high up in the air and told me, "you were a bad cat for scratching Thor."

"Humph" I thought, "that's what he gets for scaring the daylights out of me, and I'm going to puke if you don't put me down."

Mary nuzzled me in the face, cuddled me back in her arms, and carried me inside the house with Thor at her heels.

She put me down on the floor, told me to be a good boy, and turned her attention to Thor. She pulled out a box of dog biscuits from the closet along with an antiseptic and proceeded to clean off Thor's nose with the stuff in the bottle and a piece of cotton, promising him a treat for being such a good boy.

I watched, snorted, and lost interest in all the attention the dog was getting. My inquisitive mind decided the house was more interesting then the shenanigans going on over a scratched nose, so I meandered out of the kitchen into the hallway. No one stopped me, so I charged off to check it out. Bolting through the dining area and into the living room, I came to an abrupt halt and crouched down.

There, lying on the couch was the most beautiful cat I had ever seen. She was pure white with silky long hair, paws relaxed, and her long fluffy tail flopped down off the couch touching the floor.

"Hello," I mewed. Nothing happened. She just continued to sleep. I howled out "hello," and she still didn't move. "What in the world is the matter with you?" I mumbled, as I slowly approached her.

Suddenly, she opened the most beautiful blue eyes I had ever seen, looked right at me and panicked. She flew up off the couch, jumped up across the piano keyboard, which made a loud drumming sound, and up onto the top of it. There she plopped, whirled around and hissed long and hard at me. I was dumbfounded and couldn't believe she was hissing at me. I turned my head around to see who else was in the room. Just as I thought, no one was there. "What is the matter with you?" I mewled.

Mary walked into the living room with Thor at her heels. "I see you've met Lady."

She walked over to the piano and picked Lady up, stroking her gently. The cat responded to her and calmed down, nestling her head on Mary's arm, but not taking her eyes off of me. It didn't seem to matter to her that Thor was also in the room.

"Lady, meet Cat. He is our new barn cat. Sweet little boy. Not much older than a kitten and he won't hurt you," Mary said as she put Lady down on the floor next to me.

She sniffed at me, watched me intently for a minute and then proceeded to lick her front paw. "I'm deaf numb nuts, and you scared me silly."

I shook my head. I realized she hadn't said anything, but I picked up her thought. "What's deaf?"

"I can't hear anything stupid. I was born that way. Goes with my beauty and coloring. That's what the mistress said." With that thought, she stood up, went over to Thor, and proceeded to rub up against him. Thor snickered at me, smiled at Lady and the two went off towards the kitchen.

"Come on Cat, let's get you something to eat too," Mary said as she walked back towards the kitchen.

I sat where I was for a few minutes, perplexed by what had just happened, thinking it out and absorbing what I had just learned. "A deaf cat whose best buddy is a dog. Now that takes the cake. Well at least we can communicate with thoughts. That's a start." I popped up and wandered into the kitchen.

Lady was sitting on the countertop, watching her mistress doing something in the sink and Thor was lying down next to the door watching the room. I walked over to the counter and jumped up next to Lady. She looked at me and thought, "what are you doing up here?"

"Watching what you're watching, okay?"

"Whatever numbskull" she said as she turned back to watch the water splashing in the sink.

"Get down children, Harry will be home soon and you know how he doesn't like you animals near his food." Mary gently pushed at Lady to get down and looked at me. We both jumped down and sat on the floor.

"How long have you lived here?" I questioned, mentally. All of my conversations with Lady were thought to thought. Her responses were also thoughts.

"Oh about 5 years now. Mistress said I celebrated my birthday about a month ago. She is fun to listen to. Her mind wanders all over the place. Sometimes I just block her thoughts out. She can make me dizzy with all that's going on. But, when it concerns me, I pay attention very carefully. She says I have beauty and a gift, and knows I can understand her. The farmer says it's her imagination, but deep in his thoughts, he knows better. He thinks she's gifted and can talk to animals, but it's only if the animal wants to talk to her."

"What about him?" I asked as I motioned my head in the dog's direction.

"Thor? He's my best friend. Lived here longer then I have and is very protective of his home. Mistress thinks he's the farmer's dog, but I know better then that. He loves our mistress dearly and he thinks his job is to protect her. He's quite smart in his own way. So what's your story?"

"Me, I was born in a garage in the city. My mama was feral, but I chose to live with a family. So, I had a home once. The father took me to jail because they moved away and the little girl cried and cried. Jail was an ugly place and I escaped. I wandered for a bit and found the barn. My name was Blackie, but the farmer named me Cat. Mama use to call me her squeaky one."

"Wow, that must have been a wild experience. Someday you'll have to tell me about your adventures. I've never been outside. I often think of what it would be like, but since I can't hear, mistress and Thor think that is very unwise."

"Outside is a dangerous place, but it's also an exciting place. The smells, the leaves, the grass, the flowers are all so beautiful. Maybe some day I'll take you out there so you can see for yourself." Then I heard myself think aloud, "I'll protect you."

"Don't give her any ideas," snorted Thor. "Mistress would get really upset if anything happened to Lady."

Mary put some food in our dishes and we all went and ate. Then Lady looked around and decided she was going to take a nap. I was too excited about meeting my new family and decided I needed to go out and potty. Thor followed me outside, watching me like a hawk.

Chapter 21

"I'm very happy Thor," I mewled when we got outside. "Lady is beautiful and I think I'm in love."

"Nonsense little boy," Thor grumbled. "Lady has been fixed and can't have any babies. When you achieve adulthood, she will not interest you anymore. Don't break her heart by vowing your love and then taking off with another female that can have kittens."

"What's fixed?"

"Fixed is when a female can't have babies and a fixed male can't make babies. I'm fixed. The farmer said it was necessary so I wouldn't wander. The vet took my gonads when I was a puppy. I've heard, if they don't, the need to make babies gets so great, that you can't control the urge to go on the prowl."

"Are they going to fix me?"

"Don't think so kid. The farmer thinks that you should make babies. Help with the work. So, I guess when you're old enough you'll find a female and set up housekeeping in the barn. Chico was the barn cat before you. He had a nice family living with him, but he got sick. The farmer decided that it wasn't safe to keep his children or his female. He was afraid they would have the same illness, so he put them all to sleep for good. The farmer called it humane euthanesia. The mistress called it murder. Boy, was she angry with him for a long time. She cried a lot too. Promised Lady and me that would never happen to us even if we did get sick also. So, barn cat, don't ever get sick. The farmer can be pretty mean that way."

I had so much to think about. My mind was going in so many different directions. I felt like I just had to get away by myself for a short while and think things out. I wished Thor a good day and took off for the barn, with its darkness and sweet smells to absorb all I had learned this day.

I found a pleasant spot in the upstairs hay, curled up and went to sleep. I had strange dreams about running through the woods fast as the wind with Lady at my side, laughing and playing along the way. Thor was there too, very serious and loping along in what seemed slow motion in the dream, but strangely keeping up with us. Then I heard the howls. Fear gripped my belly, my whiskers twitching and all I wanted to do was run faster away from the howls, but to my dismay, I knew I couldn't leave Lady and Thor behind to fend for themselves. The dream went on and on with the howls and fear until I woke up and realized the howls were real. Still at a distance, but I could hear them nonetheless.

I sat up and realized the fear was real too. My subconscious was warning me. Quite agitated, I prowled the barn, checking on the cow and her heifer. All was well with them as she chewed her cud and the baby nursed, seeming oblivious to the sound penetrating the walls of the barn. The knot of fear in my belly wouldn't go away.

A mouse wandered into my peripheral vision, stopped and twittered a bit. Now, I felt fear emanating from the creature. In one motion of muscular beauty, I pounced, breaking its neck in one bone crunching clutch of my mouth.

The fear in me made me angry and instead of ending the battle and removing the mouse from my barn, that feeling in my belly made me, vicious and wild. I tore the mouse to shreds, clawing and ripping until all that was left was tiny pieces of animal spread all over the floor of the barn leaving a stain of red as if someone had taken a can of red paint and splashed it all around the place.

When all was said and done, I was panting and howling without even realizing I was doing it. My howls turned into tears of anguish and I lay down and sobbed for what seemed like hours. Control started coming back into my mind as I laid there wondering why I did such a thing. Now I had a filthy stain and smell of death in my ordinarily immaculate barn. Slowly, I got up and started taking the pieces of mouse outside and buried them in a hole I patiently dug in the mud. One by one, trip after trip, I walked without so much as a whimper or thought. After discarding the remains, I cleaned the mess with my tongue, and ate the smaller pieces I did not bury. Then I scratched hay across the spot until I could no longer see any residue of what I had done. I could still smell the mouse on the boards of the barn floor, so I sprayed my own scent until all I could smell was myself. Then I recovered the spot with fresh hay and wandered off to clean the reeking smell of dead mouse off my body.

Bathing myself and concentrating on what I was doing, my ears still listened, hearing the howls of the coyotes. My subconscious monitored the sound, adjusting the tone for distance and I knew that they were quite a distance away, and not a threat to my well being for now. My bowels were cramping, so I went outside and pottied on top of the remains, and covered that. Standing straight up, tail high, I let the hairs on my body feel the air to reassure myself that those evil creatures were not within my feeling distance.

All I felt was the stirring of the air from the trees, and smelled the sweet promises of a warm summer. Back in the barn, I again did my rounds to assure myself all was still well. Then I curled up in one of my favorite spots and slept the night away. My subconscious stayed more alert then ever, listening to the sounds of the night, noting that it started to rain.

Part IV

Adulthood

Chapter 22

The next few days were dreary and gray, raining off and on, so I hung around the barn checking every nook and cranny, watching the farmer and his workers do their chores. At night, I prowled listening to the distant howls and the grumbling sky. There was a craving, a yearning awakening in my young body that I did not understand. I felt so antsy. Catnaps were my specialty those few days, not going into a deep and restful sleep, but rather drifting in and out of semi-sleep, crouched into an escape position on my belly with legs curled under me and tail tucked tight, head up, eyes closed. Definitely not restful, so I would yawn and stretch, roam around the barn, nibble on my food and then resume my semi-alert position.

Finally, the rains and gray ended on the morning of a magnificent sunrise, the sky aglow with reds and shades of gold. I wandered over to the yard and jumped on the fence, waiting for Thor to come out. Thor, to my surprise was in his doghouse, mumbling and grumbling in a dream. I jumped into the yard and ambled over to Thor. "Hey dog, are you awake?"

"Go away cat, can't you see I'm sleeping," growled the big shepherd.

"Oh come on Thor, don't be an old grouch. It's going to be a beautiful day. Sun's out and the air is warm."

Thor opened one eye and looked at me. "Hmm," he thought, "he looks like he grew in the last few days."

Pulling his big body out or the doghouse, Thor wandered a bit, found a place on the fence, and lifted his leg. I watched thinking he's never gonna stop peeing.

Then he sauntered over to the back porch where his water dish was and lapped a big drink. I meandered over, smelled the water and took a few courteous sips realizing I was thirsty also.

Thor sat down and scratched, then stretched, and walked back over to the fence and lifted his leg again.

"How come you're sleeping in your barn instead of the house," I asked, as I trotted along, keeping up with the old dog.

"Was just such a beautiful night once the weather cleared. Felt as if I needed to stay out in my doghouse and enjoy the air. Anyway, I heard the coyotes howling last night and I just got restless. I get these feelings as if I'd like to run with them, but it passes. I just needed to be out."

"Run with them? They damn near killed me. One really evil coyote found my den and chased me. I could smell and feel his hot rank breath on me. One more second and I would have been his dinner."

"How'd you escape little cat?"

"Climbed a tree. Pure luck it was there. Climbed so high I thought I'd never get down. Thought he'd never leave either. And don't call me little."

Thor snorted, and as they wandered around the yard, the big dog told me about coyotes.

"They're part of the dog family ya know. Distant cousins to the wolves. I heard they are much bigger here in the northeast than they are anywhere else in this country. Some say, they mated with the red wolf years ago and gained his size along with his intelligence and cunning. Problem with coyotes is they have a mean and evil streak in them when it comes to other animals. Can never be tamed or be friends with anyone. It's their mating season now. That's why they've been howling so much. If I wasn't fixed, this is the urge that I mentioned, and I would most likely be wandering looking for a female. Their mating call is so strong that it sends desires through me that I can never satisfy, but the call is so enticing." Thor sighed very loudly and shook his head. "Enough fantasizing ... I don't really want to be out there. I've got a very good life here."

"I felt it too," I mumbled. "It's a call, a yearning, an urge, a need that seemed to get stronger the more they howled. I felt as if I wanted to wander off somewhere to find a meaning to this strange feeling even though the coyotes terrify me. Is it because I'm not fixed?"

"Yes, litt ... ..., I mean, yes cat. Eventually you will give in to these urges to wander, and will find what you are looking for."

"Thank you for helping me understand whatever it is I'm looking to understand and for not calling me little."

Thor smiled down at the little cat. "Hey, ya want to see my dog house?"

I was amazed how small the dog house was for such a big dog. After all, my barn was bigger than the house and it was all mine to roam around in. But, I realized it was special to the old canine and decided it best to tell him how wonderful it was.

Thor and Cat bonded this day. It wasn't earth shattering or even spoken out loud, but it was felt deep in the soul of each animal. They knew instinctively they would be fast friends forever.

Chapter 23

"There you are little Cat. I was up at the barn calling you for breakfast, and here you are hanging out with Thor." Mary was walking across the yard, spotted me and the Thor meandering around the dog house. "Why don't you both come in and say good morning to Lady. She was staring out the window with such a wistful look. I was wondering why. Now I know. "Come on boy," she said to Thor. To Cat, she called "kitty, kitty, come on kitty, kitty."

I looked at Thor and mentally questioned,."What's this kitty, kitty stuff?"

Thor just shrugged and responded, "That's just her. Thinks it's endearing."

We followed her into the house, Thor first with wagging tail and goofy look on his face. I followed, tail high with a slight curve on the top, signifying my happiness.

Lady met us at the door, peeking over the threshold. Mary bent down and shooed her inside. She tried to ignore her, but the woman was too much of an obstacle, so Lady backed off until both of us were in the house. Then she followed us across the floor sniffing at me with a lot of intensity.

I side stepped her attention a couple of times, then mentally asked, "what are you doing?"

"You smell more like a man than a boy," she said. "I just wanted to make sure you were the same cat. You certainly do smell good," she purred."

We heard Thor snicker as he pretended to be eating from his bowl.

That early morning was a fun time for me. Lady took me around the whole house and showed me her hidey holes, her toys, and where she slept. After investigating every nook and cranny in the farm house, we curled up on the bed that Lady slept in, bathed one another other and talked.

"What is it like outside? I've never been out there. I smell the sweet and acrid fragrances when the doors and windows are open, and I yearn to feel the grass on my paws and belly that Thor talks about. I feel the warmth of the sun when I lay by the window and can feel the wind when it blows like little whiffs of cold sneaking in under and around the panes of glass. Does the sun have sound? I know the rain and wind do from vibrations I feel. There are other strange feelings too. Distant vibrations that scare me, and twittering vibrations from bugs and birds that tickle me and make me giggle."

I thought awhile and remembered things my mama had told me, and the things I had encountered in my young life. I thought about the bad people I met and the good people. I thought about the coyotes and shivered thinking that if she were out there with her deafness, surely they would have had her for dinner.

Finally I answered her. "It is very big out there, both beautiful, and ugly. The grass and sun are good things. Nothing better then rolling in some grass, then chasing a butterfly or a moth on a warm sunny day. The cold rain and ice are bad things. They make you shiver and if you can't find shelter from the winter wind, you can die. The world has good people like your mistress, who will treat you with nothing but kindness and love, but there are bad people too who are evil and mean and will try and hurt you. There are good animals like Thor who are friendly and helpful and bad animals like the coyotes that would eat you for dinner.

You need all your skills to survive out there. You can't hear Lady. Maybe some of your other senses have made up for some of your deafness, but still you would have a major handicap. Your mistress is right. You are much safer here in the house with your toys and your rays of sun, than outside."

Her eyes welled up with tears, and I thought I had said something terribly wrong. Upset with myself, I started to lick her tears away begging her to forgive me for being so rude.

Instead, she thanked me for being so honest. "That's mostly what Thor has told me. It is too dangerous for me outside. I understand this, but sometimes I just want to feel all that you feel out there before I get old and die. I want to feel the grass on my belly, just once."

We laid there together for a while and the warmth of each other's bodys put us to sleep. I dreamed of running like the wind with Lady at my side. Lady dreamed of rolling in the grass with the blades tickling her belly with me watching over her safety.

# Chapter 24

With spring moving into summer, the whole world came alive and speeded up. First the early flowers, the daffodils and hyacinths, exploded in colorful decorations in the mistress' garden. The grass turned green and started to grow. The trees stood tall and shook their branches at the sun, popping buds, the forsythia opened its butter golden buds, and before one knew it, the world had turned from drab grays and browns to rainbows of color.

The birds started their nests and their early morning and evening chatter, and the mice in the barn started having babies and I was quite busy keeping them under control. With the abundance of life came the yearning inside of me. At times it became overwhelming and I would sit in the hay loft at night, looking out at the sky and howl incessantly. My song was the song of lonesomeness, the need for a mate.

One night, I heard a response, coming from quite a distance, but an answer nonetheless. I flew down the stairs of the barn, out the door, across the field and up on the back yard fence. I sang my heart out and then waited for the response. It came. A little closer then before, as if the other singer was working itself towards me. Across the yard I flew, up onto the other side of the fence singing away.

The response was coming from across the next field and closer, definitely female. My heart twittered, my jowls expanded and I headed full throttle towards her song.

Leaving cautiousness behind, I ran across the field, every hair on my body alert with expectation. Just as I was close enough to see the shadow of her body, another cat appeared. This one definitely was male and responding to the same drive. I stopped dead in my tracks and lay down in the grass, ears and whiskers fully extended, tail and nose twitching.

The other male had not spotted me. He was bigger, most likely a full grown animal of definite determination. Totally oblivious to anything but the smaller female shadow, he stalked her as she made her way in my direction.

"Come here my pretty one. Make me a happy male," the stranger purred as he followed her.

I could smell both of them. She had the sweet odor of a young innocent female, something like Lady, but much much stronger. He had the nasty rank odor of the feral cats at the cat prison. The estrogen smell of the female in heat was a perfume that made strange yearnings take over my common sense. No longer was I, the conservative cautious one. I was a male Tom with overpowering desires, determined to satisfy them.

I watched the big male getting closer and closer. The young female stopped and turned around to look at him. She didn't like his smell. It was the fragrance of meanness and his eyes looked evil. "Please leave me alone," she begged.

"No, no, my little one. I found you and I am going to make you mine. I'm hungry with desire for you and I will have you."

The little female backed up, eyes full of fear and loathing, breathing quite heavily and crying ever so softly, knowing her fate had been set. She knew she was in heat and would conceive babies, but dislike for this male was so strong, she contemplated fighting him to the death. Maybe, just maybe, she could hurt him enough to get away.

Suddenly I appeared. I rose up out of the grass, jowls swollen, all the hair on my body standing up, ears forward, tail straight out behind, making me as big as possible, and growling deep from the stomach. I sidestepped the young female and eyed in on the ugly male with total concentration.

Caught unawares, the big male laid his body down on the ground; ears pinned back and growled a guttural cry back at me.

I pounced as I would on my mice prey, mouth opened, ears back, lips pulled back from my teeth and bit down on the neck of the ugly one as deep and as hard as I could. The big cat roared in pain and rolled with me on his back. Over and over we rolled, with all claws flailing and fur flying, screaming at one another. I was raked across the back breaking the skin, but would not let go my death grip on the back of the other cat's neck. Deeper and deeper I sunk my teeth, almost oblivious to the pain from my wound. Finally, the big cat broke loose, and swirled around, catching me on the tip of my right ear with his teeth and bit down. I wrenched away and again, was on the big cat's back, legs wrapped around its underbelly, claws raking and digging, teeth biting down deep on it's neck again, causing a new wound.

As suddenly the fight started, it ended. The big cat went limp under my weight and screamed. I rolled off and spun around ready to attack again, but the big cat rolled over on it's belly showing true submission and fear in it's eyes, then rolled back over on its stomach and crawled a distance.. Then he got up on all fours, tail tucked between his legs and slinked off into the night mumbling how he would someday get even.

I sat down and started cleaning the other cat's blood off my paws, keeping my eyes alert to the darkness in the direction the other cat had gone.

"You're bleeding," said the female, as she came close and started licking my wounds.

"My wounds can wait. We must get out of here just in case there are others." With that, we ran across the field together, hopped the fence into the back yard, went over the other side of the fence and into the barn.

Chapter 25

"Stay here," I said, and went back outside to survey my territory. All was quiet. I sprayed the ground around my entrance and then went back inside to introduce myself to the beautiful young lady I had so dramatically saved.

"My name is Cat. What's yours?" was all I could think of to say.

She smiled at me quite demurely, putting her head down, and looked at me sideways. Whisking her tail slowly and breathing in my healthy strong male odor, she replied. "I was told I am a Calico colored cat, so my mama named me Cally."

I was so nervous. Between the adrenalin rush of fighting the feral Tom and Cally's nearness, I kept moving around in a circle, checking out absolutely nothing.

Cally noticed my water dish and went over for a drink. "If I may?" she asked.

"Of course you can. I'm thirsty also." We both started sipping at the fresh water and as we did, I started to relax, and sat down, watching her from the side.

As we both came up from drinking, our noses touched, and every fiber of my body tingled to the point that I couldn't sit still for a second more. "Come on, let's go," I chirped, and flew up the stairs to the hay loft. Cally smiled and followed, knowing that she was quite happy with her pick of males. She realized I was as young as she was, and smelled wonderfully healthy.

When we reached the hay loft, I busily scratched some fresh hay onto my bed. She also noticed I was bleeding quite heavily from the cuts on my ear and back. I, on the other hand was quite oblivious to my wounds. My sex drive had taken over.

Lying down on the fresh hay, Cally suggested I sit with her and let her clean my wounds.

Obediently, I lay down next to her and she proceeded to lick my cuts clean. Next thing I remembered, we were making love. In fact, we made love several times that night. Finally, exhaustion overcame us and we both fell into a deep restful sleep, curled up in each other's warmth. As I was drifting off to sleep, I was remembering Lady's soft and sweetly scented body.

I awoke to the sound of Mary calling me to breakfast. I went to get up and was hit with overwhelming pain. Every muscle in my body ached and my ear and back were throbbing unmercifully.

Cally awoke immediately and flew over to the landing and looked down. "There's a lady putting a fresh bowl of food down, calling your name." Cally meowed a "good morning", and ran down the stairs, over to the bowl and dug in, ravenously hungry.

I crawled to the edge and looked down at them. I started piecing my fight together in my mind, and realized I must look as much of an eyesore as I felt. I mewed a "good morning," and then went back to my bed to rest some more.

Mary was concerned but smiling. "Good morning little girl," she said, as she bent down and petted Cally. "I see Cat has found himself a mate. You are a pretty little girl with all your orange, brown and yellow patches. Not more than a kitten yourself."

Cally purred away, very content to be filling her belly and have this nice lady stroking her back.

"Now, let's see what's wrong with Cat." Mary went up into the hay loft, and found me curled up in my hay. She sat down on the floor and started petting me. I moaned from the touch, it hurt so much, but I knew she meant no harm and nudged my head into her lap.

As she stroked me, she checked my wounds. "Poor little boy. You had to fight for your lady. Thor heard the ruckus and was barking up a storm. I let him out into the yard and then I heard all the noise. That must have been some fight. Let me see you cuts."

She checked me all over and determined there were only two major bites, one on my back and one on my ear, and several small puncture wounds that looked like claw marks scattered around my body. "Oh dear, I can only imagine what the other cat is suffering if you are this much of a mess and won the battle."

Mary called Lady's vet, different from the animal doctor used by her husband. Knowing Harry's fear for his cattle, she decided that I was going to be safe from any irrational fears of infectious disease and given a chance to stay as the barn cat and see the little Calico's babies born.

She put me in the cat carrier and drove me to the doctor's office. I hurt too much to panic about the situation, but my mind kept whirling around the thought that she too may be sending me off to prison or worse because of my fight. But the doctor was very gentle checking over my wounds and gave Mary some medicine and ointment. Off we went in the car again and back home. I was so happy to see my barn that I began to purr and knead the towel on the bottom of the carrier.

Oh, the medicine tasted foul, but Mary was insistent on getting it down my throat two times a day. She'd wrap me in a towel, and cuddle me on my back in the crook of her arm. Then she'd force the hideous tasting stuff down my throat. I knew in my heart she was just helping me get better, but I couldn't stop myself from fighting her. Then she'd put me down and get out the ointment. That wasn't so bad. It helped sooth the soreness of my wounds and I healed quickly.

Chapter 26

I stayed in the barn during the week of recuperation. I really didn't feel up to much of anything. I slept a lot dreaming of my lovemaking, but my mind mixed Cally and Lady together. Cally took over the barn chores and would come and lay down next to me whispering sweet thoughts as she cleaned my wounds.

I started to feel better, my appetite came back, and my desire to show Cally my world and my friends highlighted my thoughts.

Off we went one sun filled morning to introduce Cally to Thor. He was delighted to have company and was a very courteous and gentlemanly dog to Cally.

Actually, Thor was happy to have me back in the yard knowing I was back to health. He showed off a bit with his ball and bone, asking Cally if she would like to visit his house. She giggled from the attention, batted at a butterfly in response and all of us trotted over to the dog house. I jumped up on the roof and surveyed my territory while Thor and Cally were investigating the inside of the small building.

My eyes caught the silhouette of Lady in the upstairs window. I smiled and jumped down. "Come on guys, let's see if Mary will let us in the big house. I have someone I want Cally to meet." The three of us bounced across the yard, up onto the porch and sat down in front of the screen door. I waited to be let in, with tail swishing, Thor woofed "hello," calling to Mary.

"Oh my! The three musketeers are looking to come in," as she opened the door.

Thor bounded in, I trotted in and Cally demurely sniffed around a little before entering. She smelled another female cat.

Lady was sitting in the foyer to the dining room, glaring at me. "What happened to your ear and who is that?" She spat the thought at me, and the sharpness of it hit me right between the eyes.

"My ear?"

"Yes stupid, your ear. You haven't been around in over a week and then you show up with her and a chewed ear. Looks like something took a bite off the tip."

"It's a scar he received saving me from an evil Tom," replied Cally. "I think it makes him distinguished and mature looking."

"I wasn't talking to you bitch," Lady hissed.

Thor and I looked at each other and Thor said, "Think ya got mate trouble my man."

Lady lay down with ears back, opened her mouth showing her teeth and hissed as hard as she could at Cally. "Get out of here now, before I claw you to death." The thought bombarded my mind, and felt like I had been punched in the stomach. Cally backed away, head down, tail between her legs.

"No fighting children," Mary warned. "Lady has to get used to the idea of the new girl".

"Don't threaten me," hissed Cally, as she backed up closer to Mary.

Because of my inexperience with females, I was quite overcome by their behavior. I walked over to Lady, laid down nose to nose, rolled over on my back and waited. Lady sat up, took a deep disgusted sigh and marched off into the living room.

I followed her asking her what was wrong. Lady herself couldn't explain it because she was also confused by the circumstances. "I feel betrayed. You are my friend and you brought another female into my home. Why?"

"Because, because, I don't know," I stammered, lowering my head, putting my tail between my legs. "I smelled her and I got these urges. Something you and I can't share. I needed to mate. I fought a big Tom for her and won. That's how my ear got this way and I know I'd do it again." Picking my head up and standing my tail as high as it would go, I growled out loud, "Why can't we still be friends? I adore you. Don't do this to me."

Lady looked me straight in the eyes and hissed back, "Go to hell!"

Mary, hearing the commotion in the living room came bounding in. "Stop it children this instant," she yelled. " And as for you Cat, if you can't be a gentleman go outside, NOW!"

I turned and sauntered through the kitchen and out the door. "What a mess," I thought. "Why can't others accept you for what you are? I am a Tom now and all who know me have to accept this." I picked up my tail, lifted my head and trotted off to the barn.

Cally was there mewing suggestions coyly at me like a minx. I mounted her and had sex to ease my aggressions. Not the lovemaking like before, but almost violently, releasing the tension which built in me from Lady's rejection of my friendship.

Chapter 27

A week or so went by, and I adjusted to not having Lady to talk with. I begrudgingly realized that some things would never be the same, and I didn't go into the house anymore.

Things started to change between me and Cally also. She no longer wanted to play the mating game, rejecting me over and over. "What is wrong with you?" I finally asked.

"My mating cycle has passed. I no longer have any desire for you. I think I'm pregnant. My mama cat told me this would happen one day. Now I have to turn inward and take care of myself. I'll come into heat again some day and we can enjoy each other then."

"What's pregnant?"

Cally looked at me dumbfounded and then started to giggle. Again she remembered what mama cat had taught her. "Toms are Toms my dear sweet angel. At first, they don't understand what they have created and are never faithful. They'll take an interest for a short while, but not for long."

"I'm going to have baby's silly boy. We made baby cats or kittens, as humans call them. My mama said it takes about a little less then two moons for them to be ready to come out into the world."

I looked at her as if she was talking another language, completely not understanding the meaning of what she was saying. "Where do they come out from?"

"My belly. They're inside of me growing. When the time comes, my mama told me that I will know what to do. It's the instinct and it's telling me I'm pregnant. I just know. Pretty soon, I will lose interest in you, then I won't want you around. It's nature. Until I go into heat again, you may even become the enemy. Both you and I cannot help this from happening."

I didn't like this idea at all and said as much, yowling and complaining like a kitten that was hungry. Cally just sat there, semi-smiling with a very wistful, far away look in her eyes. Then she turned her back on me, wandering towards the nest, swishing her tail and hips. "Please, just go away."

Afraid that I might bite or claw her because of anger, I turned and stormed out of the barn. I proceeded to spray everything is sight, screaming quietly, in my head, about life not being fair until the anger dissipated. I then ran to the front yard, jumped up on the fence and yowled for Thor.

Napping in the shade of his dog house, Thor opened one eye and glanced in my direction, thinking "what in the world is his problem now?" Getting up, he stretched his lanky shepherd body and yawned, then trotted over to where I was on the fence.

"What in the world are you yelling about cat? I may be getting up there in years, but I ain't deaf yet."

"Lady doesn't want to be my friend anymore, Cally just about kicked me out of my own nest, and told me to get lost. What is the problem with these females anyway? I did nothing to deserve this."

Thor sat down with a giant sigh, looked down at the ground as if he was watching something intently, and didn't answer right away.

"Don't tell me you're going to give me the cold shoulder too, you dumb dog."

"Hold it you alley cat bag of bones, I needed a moment to think before I answer. You did nothing wrong, but everything wrong. It's a simple fact of nature. You, are no longer a cute male kitten with an inquisitive mind. You are a mature male Tom and females instinctively know you can no longer be trusted. You will roam for miles, fight other males, make love with other females, and may even try and kill your own male children and try and make babies with your own daughters. It's a fact of life for you son. The ladies know this and sever the ties before anyone gets hurt."

"But that's not me Thor. It's just not me."

"But it is you. The laws of nature will prevail. Always do."

"You're lying to me you stinking bag of flea bitten dog poop. Lady will take me back, you'll see," I hissed, as I jumped off the fence and strode up to the door of the house, sat down and waited for Mary to let me in.

When she opened the door to come out and call Thor for lunch, I gave her one of my wistful looks and asked to come inside. "Meow, please?"

"I just don't know. For some reason Lady was very moody after you left the last time. It's taking her a while for her to get back to her old self. But well, sure, why not? She could always use some companionship."

In I scooted calling Lady's name loudly, listening for a response.

"I'm right here numb nuts. What is your problem?"

I poured my heart out to her, telling her what Cally had said, what Thor had said, and kept repeating, "That is just not me. You know that Lady, it's just not me."

"Cally is going to have babies? Real live little kittens? How exciting for her. I can't wait to see them. Hope my mistress lets her back in the house again so I can apologize for being so mean."

Then she got this wistful sad look to her eyes and said, "I can never have my own because I was fixed, but what fun it will be to be an aunt."

"What? What are you talking about? Didn't you hear anything else?" I hissed.

Lady smiled her smile, rubbed up against me, and I went dizzy from the affection, and said. "Of course I did my dear. But, you are who you are and you are now a Tom. There is no trusting you anymore and what will be will be. You will always be in my heart. The time has come and gone for us to be best friends."

With that, she turned around and walked from the kitchen into the bowels of the house. Turning, she said, "Please don't follow me. You can't be part of my life anymore. Go!"

I was enraged and hurt all at the same time. I let out such a loud howl, Mary came running. "Out of the house now you bad boy. Scaring the be-Jesus out of me like that. I thought something bad happened."

"Fine, I'm going for good." Like a flash, I flew out of the house down the steps, paused in the yard for a minute looking for Thor. Once I spotted him, I bounded over and got right in his face.

I took Thor by surprise, and he barked a warning, not realizing that it was me for a second.

"You too Thor? I came to say goodbye to a friend, and instead I'm told to watch out. Well, have it your way, I'm leaving for good." I jumped up and over the fence and stalked into the woods without a backward glance.

Thor realizing what happened, jumped up on the fence and yelled out to his buddy, with tears in his eyes, he hollered, "Don't go, wait and think about what you're doing. You are still my friend."

I didn't even look back. I winced when I heard the words don't go, but I was so angry at everyone, I wouldn't stop, and continued on.

"Goodbye friend. I will miss you dearly," mumbled Thor, as he watched the young cat stalking off into the woods.

Chapter 28

Weeks passed and no Cat. Cally started getting fat and lazy, not bothering to hunt because food was so plentiful from Mary.

Every time the Harry went into the barn, he sounded irate and mumbled all the time about the stupid mice. Even Mary had to listen to him at the dinner table complaining about that dam Tom who didn't know when he had it so good.

Thor became morose and very quiet during the day, not eating right and spending a lot of time in his dog house with a worried look to his face. At night he would stand at the fence and howl into the woods, "Come back Cat, I miss you."

His howling kept waking Harry and Mary up the middle of the night, only to have the farmer come out into the back yard and yell at Thor, telling him he was a stupid mutt and to shut up. Thor would yell back, "I'm not stupid. I want my friend back."

After barking at his master, he would turn and howl once more, then drop down and slink back to his dog house, whining under his breath, to lay there and pout for the rest of the night. In the mornings, Thor would stand up at the fence and sniff the air, looking for signs of Cat.

Mary became edgy and nervous, and would jump at the slightest noise. She was also quite worried about Lady. The cat would sit for hours staring out the window, only picking at her food. It was almost as if she was crying constantly. Her beautiful white fur on her face had dark brown wet stains going from the corners of her blue eyes down to the edge of her little black nose. Taking her to the vet, Lady was diagnosed with a possible minor eye infection and she gave Mary some cream to put in the corners of her eyes once a day. But, it didn't help because Lady was crying and pining for her dear friend, wishing and waiting for him to come back to the farm. He was her joy in life, as she watched him intently from her window perch, and running through the grass. The happiness of watching him chasing butterflies, sitting on the fence talking with Thor, chasing birds, rolling in the grass had become part of her life. She vicariously, shared the joy with him of being outside and free. She no longer had that now, and everyday she'd wait patiently, pining in her sadness, wishing him back again. She had been so mean to him. He was gentle and thoughtful, not at all mean or arrogant like most Toms. He could never be that way, no matter what the nature of the beast. "I miss him so much," and then she'd cry.

Cally, forgetting Cat completely, knew her time was getting close, and started to reinvent her nest, making it deeper, larger and much more comfortable. Then one night, the pain of contractions came. Mama said it would be this way. Then she would push and the babies would come out, one at a time. Each and every one of them would be in a sack. She would have to break the sack with her teeth and clean the baby to make it breathe. And this she did. A total of six. She spent the better part of that night giving birth and cleaning them, making sure they were breathing. Then she cleaned up the blood and afterbirth from herself, which made her start lactating. The babies latched on to her teats and drank deeply. Cally closed her eyes and rested, content with her new role in life as a mother.

Chapter 29

I was just so confused and angry, that even though I heard Thor, I kept stomping into the woods mumbling to myself in a mewling sound, spraying every other tree trunk along the way.

"Why is fate being so cruel to me?" Thinking back over what his mama had told him about growing up to be a Tom and wandering forever, fighting for his harem, never having a home, only temporary places to rest along the way, I felt so sad and angry at the same time. I remembered the overwhelming feelings that came over me when I smelled Cally for the first time, and the fight with the evil smelling Tom. "I don't smell like that, and I am not evil," I howled at the forest. But my yearning for Cally was so great, nothing mattered except to fight for her. I thought, at that time, of nothing else but to mate with her. "Nature," I grumped, "Sucks. I would give my life for Lady and Thor if need be also, and yet, they all have rejected me."

I thought about what Thor had said, "You have become a man now, and you are what you are." Over and over these thoughts ran through my mind as I wandered, making more noise then a human mashing through the woods.

"What is your problem feral? You squeak like something that needs to be oiled. Get yourself killed out here. Dinner for someone, if you keep that up."

"Whoa, who is that? Where are you?" Lost in my thoughts, and definitely not being cautious, I was caught by surprise. Bringing myself back to the present, I went on full alert spinning around looking for where the voice had come from.

"I'm over here squeakin' feral, by the rotten log getting myself a snack. Don't get too close or I'll spray you, and then you'll stink for a long time like hot tar on a summer's day. I have no intention of being your meal for the day."

I whirled around staring at the log, went low to the ground, whiskers, ears and eyes at full alert.

From behind the log a head, the size of mine, popped up covered in soft black fur, with a bright white stripe starting at it's forehead going along the back of it's head. Then a clawed paw raked the top of the log, and the creature stood up leaning against the log sniffing the air. "Where did you go squeakin' feral? I can smell and feel you there, but I can't see you."

I started going through the files, in my head, on what I had learned about the creatures in these woods, and then I remembered. "Skunk!"

Thor was sprayed by one once, and told me the story on a lazy summer's day.

He was a puppy at the time, eager to be friends with anything that came within playing distance. A movement near the tree line caught his interest. Tail wagging, eager to see if it could be a new friend, he wandered over to the trees.

The farmer said, "No boy, you come," and ambled towards the barn.

Thor stopped, looked at his master, again at the woods and debated in his puppy mind, what would be more fun? Meeting and playing with a new friend won out. With a bark and a wag, he raced off after the creature he saw rambling along. When he reached it, he started jumping up and down, tail wagging. circling the skunk, barking, "play with me, play with me."

It was handsome full grown skunk, with pitch black fur with an astonishing iridescent glowing white stripe down it's back running from forehead to tip of it's long fluffy tail, stopping in it's tracks and whirling around. "Get lost dog," it hissed venomously. "Don't bother me."

Thor, not to be denied a new friend, became more aggressive, running in and out at the creature while barking, "let's play, let's play."

At first, the skunk did not spray. Instead, it rose up on it's hind legs, waved it's mighty paws with huge claws in Thor's face and swiped him right in the nose. His drew his lips back over his long sharp fangs and hissed again, "Get away dog, I'm warning you."

Thor yelped in pain, sat down for a second, and growled, "I didn't come out here to fight idiot, I just wanted to play, but if that's the way it is. He got up, teeth bared, growled and went in for the attack."

The skunk whirled around, raised it's fluffy black and white tail and sprayed Thor, right in his open mouth, and face.

Thor jumped in agony, swinging his head around, rubbing it with his paws, yelping in pain. "It's burning my eyes. "I can't see, my face is on fire," he howled insanely as he ran blindly back towards the sounds of his master calling him.

"Oh Jesus, what did you do Thor? Skunk of all things."

The burning just wouldn't seem to stop, and he realized there was this pungent, despicable odor in his nose. He swatted at his nose, cried unmercifully in a loud whine, trying in vain to rid himself of the putrid smell.

What a job cleaning him up. Over and over, the farmer squeezed a fluid from a sponge into Thor's eyes and washed his nose and face. Thor, lying there, whining and begging something fierce for the farmer to make the pain go away. Eventually, the burning started to subside, and although Thor's eyes were puffy and the whites of his eyes beet red, the pain started to ease, and he could see again. The smell though. That was making him ill to his stomach.

Both man and beast had baths in the special liquid soap that day. Thor first and the Harry in a big tub in the back yard.

For the most part, Thor smelled much better, and almost sweet from the shampoo, but the smell lingered in his nose for almost a week, and everything he tried to eat tasted like that malingering bad smell, and he puked a lot. Thor never forgot his encounter with the skunk that day and told his story to whomever would listen.

I never forgot this story, and mewled out loud, "Thank you my friend for sharing."

Looking at the skunk, I said, "I won't bother you polecat. Do your thing, I'm just passing by."

The skunk popped his head up again. "How'd you know my name squeakin' feral? I didn't tell it to you, but that's me, Polecat. I am so ornery, and can hurt you so badly, that nothing in these woods messes with me. Well, one enemy, that's it."

"What's that?" I was just mesmerized by the thought that skunks have such powers. My inquisitive mind kept me there to ask the question.

"Something you should be afraid of also. The great horned owl. He just loves skunk. Can't smell worth a damn, but can see the whole world from up high, like the raptor he is. Usually just goes for the babies of my species, but if he's hungry enough anything, even someone our size is fair game."

"I have no fear of birds Polecat. They fear me. What are you eating?"

"Grubs, delicious snack."

"You should be afraid. They move so fast, it's hard to get out of their way and you'll become his dinner. Now go away, and stop squeaking at me. I've got things to do." The skunk started to amble away.

Cat stalked him for a while, deadly silent, wondering what Polecats do with their time. The skunk knew he was there and started to get annoyed, stopped and turned around.

Polecat knew the cat was there, and would need the cat closer and in his line of vision in order to spray him, but at the same time didn't feel any threat and thought it unnecessary. The feral was just annoying and not dangerous.

With that thought in mind, Polecat suddenly went into high attention. Above his head he heard the busy buzzing of bees. Made his stomach growl in anticipation.

He climbed the tree towards the sound, and hanging from a thick branch, not too far from the ground was a honey bee hive.

I was amazed that this seemingly lumbering creature could climb so well, and bellied closer to the tree. Without any hesitation, and with very little finesse, the skunk reached out with one paw and dug into the hive with those massive claws and yanked. It came lose with a cracking and insane buzzing noise. Grabbing it with teeth and claw, the skunk carried it down from the tree and started ripping it apart, eating honey and bee alike, with no fear of being stung whatsoever.

Chapter 30

The bees that escaped were in a wild frenzy looking to attack anything or anyone that was within reach, and that included me.

Realizing danger, I jumped up and bounded in the opposite direction as fast as my speed could muster. I had outraced most of the bees, but not all. Some honey bees caught up with me and descended, stinging me in their death dance anywhere they could find contact. My fur protected most of my body from the danger of those stings, but my nose and ears was quite vulnerable, and they stung me, and stung me good.

I yowled in pain, the sound echoing through the woods. I knew it was dangerous to my safety to be so noisy, but I couldn't help myself. The pain of those stings on my sensitive nose and ears was almost too much to bear. Eventually, the attack ceased and I laid on a bed of old leaves, lungs heaving, trying to catch my breath, and at the same time the pain coming from my ears and nose vibrating with every beat of my heart.

I laid there for a while, mewling and cleaning, trying to get rid of the horrible stinging sensation. After a while, it eased up a bit, but my nose felt funny. I couldn't seem to breath out of it too well, and smells were muted to indistinct odors.

This feeling lasted about two days. Little did I know my nose, from the stings, had swelled up to about three times it's size and my ears were full of lumps and bumps. My cheeks were also puffed up from the bees, and I would rub them up against rocks and trees, to ease the pain. As I healed, I realized rubbing my jowls against hard objects not only felt good, but left my odor where I rubbed.

I found something new and exciting in myself. I have glands in my jowls that leave an odor behind that cannot be smelled by humans, but only other cats, telling the others that this was my territory and stay away.

During this time, I stayed close to the ground and was very cautious. My instincts told me, I was very vulnerable to predators because of my lack of smell from the swelling. I meandered along and slept close to a stream, drinking when thirsty and realized the cold water eased the pain in my nose. Slowly, but surely, all my senses returned, making me a deadly predator again.

By the third day, I was famished, and heard the rustling of a field mouse. I went into attack mode, whiskers sensing, making my strange noise that mesmerized my prey. Just as I was about to pounce, I heard this whirring noise above my head. Louder, and louder until suddenly this great bird with it's massive wings, came down right in front of me, talons outstretched, hitting the mouse dead on, digging those huge claw like needles into the flesh of the small animal. It hesitated a moment, staring me straight in the face, with those huge, round, amber, all seeing eyes, and a let out a guttural scream. "Fear me feral, because you could be next on my menu."

Then, with a couple of massive swoops of those magnificent feathered wings, he went into the sky above the tree tops in one graceful movement and flew away.

I was awestruck and speechless. That must be the raptor Polecat spoke about. I now understood the skunk's fear of this huge feathered creature. Although I had experienced other hawks before, this was my first encounter with the great horned owl, and remembered Cally and their future babies with concern in my heart. I shook the thought out of my mind. "Not my problem anymore," and trotted on looking for the highway.

Chapter 31

I found the road eventually and was surprised by it's size and length. A wide smooth black line, with white stripes and dashes meandering across the land as far as my eyes could see, cutting the country side in half. I didn't venture out onto it, but followed alongside, through the woods.

Vehicles phished by at some phenomenal speed heading in both directions. I had seen roads before, vaguely remembering the city streets where I was born, and of course, the bumpy roads at the farm. How rapid these vehicles were traveling and the size of some of them is what amazed me. It also scared me when I thought of what my friends from the woods had told me. Life could be snuffed out so quickly on this road, and I suddenly understood and felt the danger.

As I trotted alongside the road, heading for the big city, my mind started to meander, thinking about Cally and future kittens, Thor, Lady, and the really nice humans that care about all of us. My reverie was suddenly interrupted.

Grazing, by the side of the road were three fully grown does. They were munching and talking in sweet musical voices. Suddenly, in their nervous and hyper way, they all looked up, staring at an unseen something across the road. One turned toward the road, and started to walk out. The other said, "I wouldn't do that. You know it's dangerous."

"Yes, but I can smell some wonderfully sweet grasses over there. Can't you smell them? The breeze is bringing that delicious fragrance from over there."

"We smell it, but we are ignoring it. It's is too dangerous to cross over. We have the same grass here, and when the breeze changes ..."

With the sentence in mid air, they all turned and stared directly at me, sitting silently watching them. Being the skittish one of the three, the one doe, who was talking about going across, panicked a bit when she saw the me and ran onto the road.

A huge lumbering truck was speeding down the highway heading straight at the young doe. Her eyes grew to the size of silver dollars as she watched it bearing down on her, and she froze. The mighty vehicle hit her with such force that she flew up in the air, bounced across the top of it a few times, and then hit the ground with a thump. The truck kept on going as if nothing happened. The doe was gone from this world forever.

I watched the accident happen, in what felt like slow motion, although it happened in the blink of an eye. The fear and surprise on the doe's face imprinted in my mind, and I howled furiously at the horror I had just seen. "I hate humans, their machines and their cruelty," I screamed. All my childhood memories flooded over me, remembering my mama, the jail, the acrid smells, the sadness of it all. I started to sob, mewling in sad and mournful unearthly moans.

"Don't cry little feral."

Shaking my head to clear my mind, I looked up. Standing there were the other does, and they were talking in unison. "We all tried, but she wouldn't listen."

"I didn't say anything, I was just watching you," I stammered.

"But you did, feral. We knew you were there for a while. We told our sister she shouldn't go across the road, and how dangerous it was. You agreed, in your mind. We heard you plain as day say, "don't do it female deer. Don't do it." We tried, but she wouldn't listen. She would not have taught her babies any different if she lived to have any. It's survival of the fittest little feral." With that, they turned and ran off into the woods, calling out as they left, "be well friend."

My energy was spent. I laid there on a bed of grass and leaves, letting a sunbeam caress and warm my body, thinking about my life. My paws felt slightly sore, something that never quite went away after the winter of my lonely travels. I checked the pads, cleaned them, and washed away the tears from my eyes. I laid my head down and drifted into a semi sleep.

During this fugue like state, my body rested, but my mind was working overtime. I remembered the warmth of friendship with Thor, the kind human, Mary and her mate, the huge snake I had killed, the lovemaking with Cally, and the sometimes painful love I had for Lady. This was my life I thought. It is special, and mama would have been both proud and happy for me. Then I heard mama say "Oh my little squeaky one, I knew you were special. Why did you throw away this wonderful life with that crazy, obstinate way of yours?"

Hearing my mama's voice, I jumped up, wide awake, and knew what I had to do. I would no longer be called Cat or Blackie or any other name chosen by others. It would be *Squeaky, my* name given to me by mama. All would know me by this name and I was going home. Back to the farm, for better or worse. That was my territory. My family and friends were my responsibility to protect and to love however nature intended.

I had been traveling for a while now, and knew the journey back would be a long one. I also sensed the weather was changing and the warm days would get shorter and cooler with winter eventually upon me again. With a look over my shoulder at the fantasy life of the big city, I turned back the way I had journeyed. my decision was made.

Chapter 33

Sensing the shortening of the days, the smell of the air, and the feel of the environment, I realized it might be quite chilly when I returned. Not counting obstacles along the way, nor even considering that I might not even survive the journey, I headed home with the determination of my stubborn and dogmatic personality.

I marched, nonstop well into twilight that evening, with the easy grace of a healthy, well muscled cat.

Stopping at a creek for a drink of water, a noise caught my attention. There by a tree trunk, was a chipmunk so busy stuffing an acorn into a hole amongst the roots, that it was oblivious to me. "Ah, an easy dinner," as I pounced. All of a sudden there was a snapping noise and my paw was caught between the teeth of a small game trap.

The pain ripped through my mind in sharp needles of agony. I tried to pull my left front leg free, but the pain got worse and the trap tightened more. Howling in screams of both anger and pain, I tried biting myself free and only succeeded in chipping a front tooth and filling my mouth with the taste of rust.

"A barking noise?" My eyes glazed with pain and fury, my mind filled with so much confusion and despair that it took the noise a while to register. Concentrating on focusing my eyes,

I saw the dog, jumping up and down, barking like it had gone insane.

"Quiet boy, I see it."

Bending down, the young man laid his rifle to the side and stroked me. "It's a cat Champ. Got caught in a trap."

I mewled to the touch, saying "Please help me, please."

The dog sat next to his master, and placed his cold nose on my face and started licking me.

"You don't want to see him die like this either, do you Champ?"

It must have been an old trap because it was so rusted that it was next to impossible to manually spring the jaws with the release buttons on it's sides. Pulling a knife out of his pocket, the young man twisted it between the jaws of the trap, until there was enough space for me to pull my leg out. Instinct made me try and run, but my injured leg had gone totally numb, and I flopped around in circles like a rag doll.

"Easy, little cat. Let me see how much damage was done to that leg."

Sitting down, with his back to the tree, the young man placed me in his lap, and felt around the injured leg.

"Lucky little guy. Nothing seems to be broken. Young cats bones are so pliable. Feels just bruised to me. A little longer, and you might have lost that leg. Think I'll take you back to the cabin for a day or two. Let it heal and see if any of the neighbors are missing their cat."

With that he, placed me in a leather bag he was carrying, closed the top, and I was trapped inside. In a state of shock from the pain and experience there was no resistance. Instead, nature gently shut down my reactions, and I curled up in the dark, rawhide place and slept.

"Damn trappers, Champ. They put these God damned traps out here and then forget where the hell they put them. I don't think they even care."

With that, the young man ripped the stake and trap out of the ground, slung it over his shoulder and dog, man, and cat headed back to the man's base.

Sitting down to dinner, Mike, a fellow Ranger, asked, "What ya gonna do with him, Danny?".

Danny was a Forest Ranger. Camp, or base, was a cabin in the woods alongside a fire tower. During shifts, four days on and three days off, Danny and Mike shared this lifestyle together, for almost three years. Both still single, late twenties, and loved the lifestyle and responsibility.

"Oh, I don't know. Take him to the Vet for a check up. If he's as healthy as he looks, get him fixed and find him a good home. He might have belonged to somebody at one time, but don't think so, now. He's had human contact, gentle enough and probably house broken, but he's an adult male and may have gone feral."

With that thought, Danny smiled and looked over at the little black panther sound asleep in a laundry basket, nestled on a soft blanket. "Son of a bitchin' trappers," he whispered half out loud.

"I agree" answered Mike. "Nothing much we can do about it though. Not as long as it remains legal to trap in this state. A fine, maybe for trapping out of season. That God damned thing was rusty as hell, and no identification."

I heard the voices from a distance through a fog. I slowly came to the surface of reality from a coma-like state; mother nature's kind way of protecting an animal in distress. I realized I was laying on something soft, was warm, smelled food and had to pee really badly. Standing up, ready to jump out of the basket, my leg reminded me of what happened. The numbness had left, and in its place there was a sharp pain running from the paw straight up my shoulder. I sat down and licked the paw, while surveying the area around myself. In close proximity to me was what looked to be a litter box. "Okay, "soft bed, litter box!" Experience told me these humans like cats, so it should be safe."

In my weakened condition and still a little confused, I decided that I had no choice but to somewhat trust these people. Gingerly, placing weight on the injured leg, I climbed out of my bed and limped to the litter box. Once done, I stepped to the floor, sat down, and said, "okay, now feed me, I'm hungry."

What the men heard was a hoarse chirp from the little cat.

"Ah, you're awake little boy," Danny said. He got up and kneeled down beside me, and stroked my head. "That was a little squeak from a big boy. You must be hungry."

Danny cut some of the chicken they had for dinner into small pieces, filled a bowl with water and put the meal down.

I devoured the chicken, and had a big drink of water. My tummy cramped from eating so fast, so it was back to the litter box. The little amount of exercise seemed to have drained my strength, so I limped back to my bed, cleaned myself, curled up and went back to sleep.

Next morning, I had a shocking experience. Instead of a good meal and some kind words, Danny scooped me up in his arms and placed me in a small cage. "Sorry boy, but your going to the Vet this morning and get checked out."

Chapter 34

`Kind words came along with a truck ride to the Vet's office, but I wasn't listening. Memories of jail came flooding back in my mind. I was howling in anger and rage with a fierce hatred for the man who had locked me in this prison.

Danny could see that hate in the cat's eyes and wondered what in the world had happened to this animal. It was something he would never know, but he could feel the wild fear like another entity in the truck. "If this animal could kill me right now, he would."

A day later, groggy and totally disoriented, I was handed over to Danny. "He's a very healthy, strong, young cat. In order to even give him a health check up and shots, we had to sedate him. Even then, he tried to sneak out when my assistant's back was turned. Well, he's up to date on shots, neutered and good to go. Be his old self in a couple of days."

"Thanks Doc," Danny said. "He's really a neat little cat. If no one claims him in the next few days, he'll probably stay at the cabin and be our mascot."

The Vet smiled and said, "good luck keeping him from leaving. If you ask me, he's on a quest of some kind."

Tired, sore, and in dire need of a warm place to stay while I healed, I stayed for about a week or so at the cabin with the Rangers. The laundry basket was my permanent bed, lots of good food, attention, and, even toys to play with, which I felt were slightly insulting. Any other cat would have enjoyed the luxury bestowed upon me and would have stayed, but not me. As much as I felt safe in my new home, my desire to get back to family and friends was a much greater need.

One morning, playing with my fake mouse and acting dumb, I saw my opportunity. As one of the Rangers opened the door and walked out, and before it could be closed behind him, I took off. I was free and on the run again.

Chapter 35

"Run, run, like the wind," is what I thought as I hightailed it out of there. I ran for a while until my injured leg started to ache, so I slowed down to a fast loping walk.

I could hear the humans calling me, and felt a tinge of sadness. "They treated me well. I could have stayed a while, but I must get home." I walked on, choosing to ignore them.

After a safe distance, I found a good hiding spot to rest. My leg was aching and I needed a rest. Snuggled down in a mini cave of rocks by a stream, I started cleaning myself and accessing my body. My hair, where the trap had bit down on my paw, was turning a patchy, silver white, in a ragged circular pattern. A unique marking, almost like a tattoo that would be with me forever. As I cleaned my underbelly, licking the healing itch of where my testicles used to be, I thought about not having them anymore. "I don't feel any different. I'm like Thor now." I remembered the conversation with my friend, and the distant yearning in Thor's eyes. A shiver went through my body as I felt a strange sadness of what once was and never will be again. "NOOOOOOOOOOOO, I howled, not me, not me," and I laid down and cried.

I slept a deep, dreamless sleep. Next thing I knew, the sun was rising, and another day was beginning. Jumping up and getting my bearings, I realized I had slept the whole night through. This in itself scared me, because of all the dangers around me now that I was out in the wild again. I didn't realize that nature was just helping me heal both physically and mentally. Sleep of this magnitude was essential in my healing process.

I drank from the stream, stretched, sniffed that air, and went into high alert. There was a scent in the air that reeked of danger and death. I crouched down and slowly inched my way forward, smelling everything in my path. The woods around me had the acrid, sour, evil odor of male coyote urine, marking the trees with its territorial malevolence. There was another smell also. The tinny, metallic smell of rabbit blood.

The smells were fresh. No more than four hours old, and my body involuntarily trembled . "Coyotes! They could have found me, and that would have been the end." I shuddered again at the thought.

Cautiously, I moved along on my journey home, thinking out my plan of action. Onward toward the farm I marched, thinking about happiness lost, warmth, comfort, friends and human kindness. All left behind because my hotheaded temper and ego had gotten in the way.

The weather was turning colder, and my main concern was safety, The nagging pain in my leg was secondary to the dangers around me. That, and the soreness around the pads of my feet where I had been frostbitten in what seem like such a long time ago. I became nocturnal, sleeping most of the day and traveling through the night. Life had taught me to be vigilant and watchful during the darkened hours.

I didn't notice that the hairs around the leg injury were growing in all gray, spots of gray hair sprouting here and there in my thick black, furred body, and one whisker had turned totally white. No longer was I the domestic well fed cat with the gentle, laughing eyes. I was aging more quickly, like an animal of the wild, and my eyes had taken on that wily feral look of mistrust.

Night after night of the howling of the coyotes was causing an irrational anger. On the night of a full moon, I climbed to the top of a rock outcropping, puffed myself up and screamed my hostile rebuttal. My high pitched roar echoed throughout the woods, and then there was total silence. With every hair standing out on my body, I listened to the lack of sound and knew the coyotes were on the hunt. They had smelled me throughout my journey, but now they had heard me. Almost feeling their rank breath and their drops of drool on my head, I snickered, "Try and get me now, you evil bastards." Quietly, I slipped into the night, blending with the shadows in darkness.

Chapter 35

During the winter months, when food is scarce, coyotes come together and hunt as packs. Like wolves, they can bring down an animal much larger then themselves. With keen sight and great intelligence, these animals can be formidable, and have been known to attack a human if hungry enough.

Unlike wolves, they carry a gene which makes them forever wild and cannot ever be domesticated. Zane, the leader the pack, in this area of the Catskills, was a prime example of this behavior. He was an exceptionally large, strong and healthy coyote, with a mean streak a mile wide, never forgiving, never forgetting, and always conquering his prey.

Prey of any kind never escaped Zane's hunting skills, except for the little feral cat that had been eluding him since last winter. He knew this feral was in his woods and obsessed with wanting the kill. With cruel force, he directed his pack to making the finding of this cat their primary goal.

Cooler weather was here, but food was still plentiful. They needed their leader to endure the hardships of the colder months, and the pack was both confused and unnerved by their leader's preoccupation.

It caused a dissension amongst the group and tempers flared. There was a lot of arguing over incidentals, with biting and growling, play fighting became real fighting, and with that, the drawing of blood. Zane and his mate, another large gray coyote, named Teeya, demanded total obedience to their leader, with force, if necessary. Zane had even wound up ripping out the throat of one of his pack to make his point. This caused a definite underlying hostility towards him, but out of fear of his strength and cruelty, they followed his orders. The blind hatred for this cat started to consume them also, hoping it would be over soon, so they could get back to the primary goal of survival through the winter.

I was very aware of the coyotes' obsession. I knew I was being stalked continuously on my travels home. I also knew that in order to make it back home, I had to stay one step ahead of this pack at all times.

Being on the constant alert was changing me. I became wilier, more cunning, and extremely conscious of my surroundings. I wasn't making good travel time at all, quitting early, climbing trees to sleep at night, rarely hunting, and always hungry. I found myself backtracking more than maybe was necessary, but considered it a safeguard to a direct scent path for the enemy. At times, I would even sneak up on the pack and watch and listen. Their verbal language was difficult for me to understand, but their body language and thoughts was very clear and unnerving. It wasn't just killing for survival, but an evil, malicious hatred of all but their kind. I was their prime target now, and this sent shivers down my spine. I trudged on, seeking my home, thinking, it would be a safe haven with the friends I loved so much, and now, a family, that I was so eager to meet. Once out of hearing distance, in a guttural growl I'd whisper to the trees, "I will teach my children how to be cautious and to fear the coyote. How to survive the woods and how evil and dangerous this enemy of all life can be."

One morning as I was stretching from my cramped position in the crook of a tree branch, I heard different sounds. Still at a distance, but definite sounds so very familiar to me. The closer I walked, the more familiar the sounds. Suddenly, I realized what

I was listening to. "Thor! Good old Thor, barking at something, telling them to behave themselves." I ran the distance towards Thor's bark as fast as I could travel, almost flying that last eighth of a mile, not caring how much noise I made.

Thor heard the branches on the ground snapping and the leaves crunching under the weight of something moving fast and looked up. I hit the top of the fence in one leap, my lungs heaving, trying to catch my breath.

At first, Thor was totally surprised and let out a low warning growl at this this animal sitting on his fence. It's a cat, he thought and suddenly a light bulb went off. "Cat, is that you? You came back? My friend, you came home." He started yelping in joy, running around in circles, jumping up and down.

Chapter 36

I was, at first, so surprised by Thor's excitement about my return that I smiled and said, 'Yes it me. Older and wiser, but home now," and so overwhelmed by that thought, and the emotions that were going on inside of myself, I started to cry.

Thor noticed, felt the sadness and relief. In his doggie best friend way, he barked gruffly, "Come down from there Cat. Let me give you a proper hello."

Jumping down from the fence onto the lawn of the back yard was an awesome feeling. It all felt so familiar and safe. Thor started nuzzling me, checking me all over, sniffing, licking and noticed my smell was different. "Still Cat, but different in an odd sort of way." Looking at me, he noticed I was much thinner, older, and had an almost feral look to my eyes.

Lying down, letting Thor do his thing, I started to purr, felt a great release of tension and closed my eyes, letting my guard go, and just enjoyed the attention of my best friend.

"Who is that Thor?"

I came to attention immediately. Opening my eyes and jumping into fight or flight mode, I found myself staring at a young bright orange tabby, not more then a kitten meowing the question.

"I should say who are you?" I hissed.

"Whoa boys, whoa!" Thor jumped between them. "This here is one of your sons. Mary gave him the name of Murphy."

"Murphy, this here is your father. He's come home."

Murphy didn't realize how close he came to being mauled by the big cat, but Thor knew and that's why he jumped between them. "Give Cat a chance to think for a minute and calm down."

To Thor I said, "My name is Squeaky, now and forever." Then turning back to the orange tabby, I hissed, "Don't come too close kid or I might scratch your eyes out." Then I sat down, make believing I was cleaning one of my front paws, while sizing this Murphy up and down.

Murphy had the common sense enough to lie down and be quiet. Instinctively he knew not to make eye contact with the big cat, knowing that was a sign of dominance and he might very well attack. Of course, he was not very happy with this intruder coming into his territory, but sitting alone with only Thor to intervene could mean he might get hurt. This he solidly knew, wishing his brother Smokey was around. Maybe together they could take him.

I had heightened my ability to read thoughts as a survival tactic against the coyotes, and knew exactly what this kitten was thinking. Looking at Thor I growled, "And who and what is the Smokey this pipsqueak is thinking about?"

Thor knowing his friend and what he might have been through, was not really surprised. He realized in the wild, the only way to survive is to know what a potential enemy is thinking. "Come my friend, we'll go over by my dog house and we'll talk about what is happening around here."

Thor started to amble away, and with one last glare at the young cat, I stalked away, following my friend towards the doghouse. Thor lay down by his water dish, offering me a drink of the fresh water and waited.

Chapter 37

I sat and listened while Thor began his story of the farm and my family and all that transpired.

"Shortly after you left, Cally's time had come. She gave birth to 6 beautiful healthy kittens, four girls and two boys. The girls looked quite like their mother, all Calico in coloring, ranging from many patches of black, orange, and white to just a few on silver gray bodies. The boys were completely different. One male was a bright orange tabby with golden eyes. The other, as black as you with startling green eyes. Mary gave them all names. You met Murphy, and will soon meet his brother Smokey. Where one is, the other is close. The girls stick close to their mama and to be honest, I forget the girls' names or else mix them up. I just never get the names straight, so Cally will have to introduce them to you."

"Murphy was the smallest kitten, born last, but the most aggressive. He gets into all kinds of trouble, always jumping into something without fear or regard of limb or life. Smokey, on the other hand, was the largest kitten and first born. He's a thinker that one, cautious and careful, all the time, thinking a situation out before committing."

"The brothers are exceptionally close, and when Murphy gets himself into an awkward position or in trouble, Smokey is always there to help get him out of whatever situation he's gotten into, no questions, and no fear."

"Murphy has a quick temper that flares easily, whereas Smokey is slow to anger. Occasionally, Smokey will get so annoyed with something his brother does, that he'll pummel the little one around. Murphy wouldn't take that from anything or anyone else but Smokey. It's amazing and funny at times, to watch Smokey bat Murphy around like he is a ball and him just taking is in stride, no claws, and no teeth. Gets up, dusts off, and goes off on another adventure."

"What about you, my friend. What has happened to you while you were gone?"

I gave him a quick summary of what had happened during my adventures, about the coyotes, the trap and the people who took me in, winding it down with the visit to the doctor and my neutering.

A light bulb went off in Thor's head and he blurted out what he realized about Cat's odor. "I knew it was you but there was something different in your odor. You smell very male and like yourself but no longer offensive to me with the smell of a Tom. This is a good thing. You won't want to roam as much and fight other Toms. Your children and Cally have been fixed also, so life around here will be easier for everyone. You'll all learn to get along with your boys and not try and make babies with your daughters. Cally and Lady have become great friends, and jealousy over you will not come between them again. Above all, my best friend will maybe stay and be happy with the wonderful life we all have here."

I thought about this, smiled a thin smile, "I don't feel any different Thor, just happy to be home." With that, I spread out on the grass next to Thor's dog house, closed my eyes and rested.

Chapter 38

While Thor and Squeaky were talking, Murphy eavesdropped on some of the conversation, and realized Thor was extremely happy to have this cat back, and actually called him his best friend. Not wanting to listen to anymore after he heard that and a little miffed at Thor for saying this animal was his best buddy, he hightailed it to the fence, jumped up and started yelling for his brother. "Smokey, where are you. I need you now. Smokey come quickly."

Smokey had been in the sunflower patch watching the small yellow finches, with their black striped wings, flitting in and out of the sunflower centers, eating the seeds, and chirping their canary sweet songs. Getting a bit bored, he started to doze and jumped to attention at his brother's loud screaming. He stretched, and took off high speed, in the direction of Murphy's howling.

He jumped up on the fence next to his brother, sat down and growled "What are you yowling about, idiot? You look perfectly alright to me!"

Murphy was so excited; he couldn't sit still while he told his brother what had happened. Around and around he circled with tail twitching a mile a minute. posturing his agitation, blurting out the story in half sentences which sounded to anyone else like a series of short chirps and grunts.

Smokey thought about what Murphy just told him and meowed, "We have to get mama and our sisters, and then go say hello."

Off they went in the direction of the barn, Murphy becoming the town crier. Yelling so loudly, that to anyone's ears he sounded like he was in dire trouble. Cally came running and as Smokey was about to tell her the news, Murphy blurted it out so quickly, his speech sounded like one giant howl.

"Slow down little son, and tell me again. You think your father is back?"

When the news sunk in, Cally called all her girls together and told them they were going to meet their daddy, and off they all went to the back yard.

One by one they jumped up on the fence; first Murphy, followed by mama, Smokey and then the girls.

Thor looked up first, and then nudged me. With sleepy eyes, I looked around and suddenly sat up straight, wide awake, staring back at all those cats staring down at me, and spotted Cally.

"Hello Cally girl. Are these all your children?" Sniffing the air, I continued, "the females look very much like you, but the males are, well, so different."

Jumping down from the fence and walking slowly towards me, she said "These are your children also."

Cally walked closer to me, laid down and coyly rolled back and fourth on her back a few times, showing both submission and welcome. "Hello Cat, are you back home for a while?"

I settled down across from her, front paws extended, head erect and watched her thinking, "She's just as pretty and sweet as the day I met her." With that thought in mind, I laid my head down and let her sidle up to me, squirming and wiggling her prone body closer and closer until at first our whiskers touched, and then our noses. Then, we were nuzzling and Cally was cleaning my ears while I purred in contentment, tail wagging up and down.

"Look at mama, Smokey. They look like they've been together forever, her making smooching noises and him sucking it up. What gives with this?"

"Get over yourself Murph. Mama likes him, and he's your father. Your sisters don't seem upset and neither does Thor. The girls are giggling up a storm and Thor looks happy as can be. It must be alright and he must be a good guy."

Meanwhile, Lady had been in the window watching what was going on outside and realized that it was Cat who had came back. Her eyes welled up with tears and the excitement and happiness of that thought overwhelmed her and she could think of nothing else but getting outside to say hello and tell him how sorry she was to treat him so badly.

She ran through the house yelling for Mary. She couldn't hear herself, so she had no idea what she sounded like, or how loudly she was yelling. What Mary heard was a cat in great distress and she came running looking for Lady to see what had happened to her. She found Lady, at the back door, scratching and pounding at the door as if the devil was chasing her and it was a matter of life and death to get out that door.

Mary bent down and scooped her up in her arms, stroking the back of Lady's head. "What's the problem girl? You've never acted like this before."

As she opened the door to get a good look at what might have her cat carrying on, Lady hurled herself forward, digging her claws into Mary's arm and projected herself right into the air, landing squarely on all fours, outside. Ducking, ears back, tail straight out, she made a mad rush all the way out into the back yard, and ran straight across the lawn. She didn't stop until she was next to Thor. Then she sat down, stunned and frozen by what she had accomplished. Never before had she felt grass under her feet or actually felt the warmth of the sun on her body, without the window. The breeze had a vibration she never sensed before, and the smells were overwhelming, both beautiful and very scary. Everything went out of her mind, and for a moment she forgot why she had run out into the yard and away from her mistress. Mary was right on Lady's tail, and scooped her up into her arms. "Naughty girl," she admonished. "Why in the world did you do such a thing?" Then she looked around, saw the strange cat, and realized it looked familiar.

"Cat is that you? Oh my God, it is! You came back. Come to the house with me so we can take a look at you."

With that, she turned around and walked back to the house with Lady in her arms. Getting to the door, she turned back and said "Hurry up, get in here, now."

They all looked, and headed for the house, Cat in the lead, then Cally and the girls, followed by the boys, then Thor bringing up the rear.

All the time they were out there, Thor felt as if something was watching them. He kept hesitating and checking over his shoulder as he walked to the house.

Although he couldn't catch a whiff of anything out of the ordinary, instinctively he had a strong feeling something was amiss outside the compound, and kept checking over his shoulder as he walked to the house.

Chapter 39

Something was watching. Zane and two of his pack were watching everything going on at the farm house from a discreet distance. Hidden in the underbrush of the woods, they sat and watched from downwind, so none of the animals in the yard could pick up any odor on the breeze and smell their presence.

Zane was salivating, and with a low growl he announced he could not wait to kill the feral cat and eat his heart. The other two looked at one another, got up and paced around in a circle, a distraught whining coming from their throat. They had been totally unnerved by their leader's obsession with this cat, and now they could see it and smell it in him stronger then ever before.

"Quiet" he growled, "they will hear you if you keep that up. We must have a plan of action. The cats will be easy prey and there are enough of them to make your kill worthwhile. The dog will be a problem, but the humans around here will be our most dangerous adversary."

He got up from his crouched position, and with one long last look at the farm house, he trotted away, with his two pack coyotes following three steps behind, wondering the whole while, what their leader planned to do.

That night, back at their den, Zane laid his plan out to the pack. They would take turns watching the farm house to watch the habits of all their prey. His first priority in his plan was the dog. He had to be the first to be taken out of the picture completely.

Once they established his daily and nightly routine, they would attack. Waiting for a dark and moonless night. Then let the fight begin. The noise from the attack would wake the humans. Before they had a chance for any kind of action, the dog had to be taken down. Then they were to run like the wind.

The humans would now be on the total alert for them, possibly even armed with shotguns. Maybe even a coyote hunt, but they would all be gone. Zane would move his pack to another area, for a little while. Then when all calmed down and the humans forgot about them, they would come back for their real prey as a full pack.

Animals don't have a sense of time as humans understand it. They move through time according to natures design. Weather changes, barometric changes, earth movement, smells and sounds in nature is how they interpret time. Cold days were ahead and the urge to kill to gorge their bellies and build body fat, as well as finding a safe, dry permanent den was all about survival and a priority to all. Even Zane in his insane state of mind felt this.

As the last quarter of moon rose that night, the coyotes howled their agreement to the pending plan, releasing their tension and cheering the happiness of knowing soon, all of this would be in the past and the kill would be theirs by design.

Chapter 40

Once inside the house, everyone was trying to talk at once. Mary was admonishing Lady about running outside; while Lady is meowing at me telling me how happy she was I came back home and how she regretted sending me away. Cally was chirping agreement with Lady and trying to introduce me to the children. The girls were yowling, asking Cally what they should be calling me. Murphy and Smokey were meowing to each other about Lady actually running outside and me just showing up out of nowhere. Thor was barking for everyone to be shut up and let one at a time speak. He was just having a difficult time translating everything they were saying at once. I was the only one not making a sound, and to anyone outside, it must have sounded like a chaotic screaming of animals and a woman in trouble.

When Harry pulled up in his truck, this is what he heard and thought something bad had happened in the house. Racing in the door, he couldn't believe what he saw. All of Mary's pets sitting on the floor making all this noise, with Mary bending over a small black cat scratching his ears while talking to Lady. Thor saw him first and ran over and in his excitement, jumped up on the farmer's shoulders, gave him a warm slurp of his tongue right across the face, and barked, "Look who came home?"

Thor never did that since he was a puppy, and was never allowed to do such a thing. He came to his senses, realized what he had done, dropped down to the floor, tail between his legs, head down and slinked away to a corner, laid down and whined "Oh boy, I'm in big trouble now."

Mary looked up, saw her husband standing there, "Harry, look who came back."

"Well, I'll be" was the only thing he could say. "He looks healthy. A little thinner, and there is something different. Look at his paw. His hair has turned white in a complete circle around it. Sure it's the same cat?"

"The other animals are sure it's definitely is him. He must have lived with someone for a while and they took good care of him. He's been neutered also."

"If animals could only talk Mary. He could tell us what has happened since he left. Anyway, he fits right in with the others being fixed and all. Welcome Cat."

After we said good night to Lady, and left the house, I stayed with Thor in the yard before heading back to the barn with the rest of the family. He told me that all my family had been fixed. Mary and Harry had discussed the idea after you left. It made sense since, with Cally had her six kittens there was no need for anymore barn cats. Once neutered, the boys would be much less likely to wander. Spaying Cally and her females would make them much more content and much less likely for some Tom to be coming around and upsetting the apple cart. So, once the kittens were old enough and before Cally went into heat again, off they all went to the Veterinary clinic.

The next few days settled into themselves in a routine sort of way, with me getting to know my family. My four girls were very much like their mother. Sweet, soft spoken, and gentle. Queenie, named because of a bright patch of oranges and brown on her head that resembled a crown, was the largest and a most colorful Calico, of the four. Then there was Tessie and Tofu who looked almost identical. Both were gray with soft, subtle patches of oranges, golds, and tans. I think Cally even had a hard time telling them apart, but she'd never say that. The fourth was Little

Paw, named for her petite size. She too, was mostly gray with subtle Calico coloring. Even though she was the smallest, she was the most feisty of the girls and, like Murphy, full of mischief. Unlike her brother, she did listen when she was admonished by Cally. It was also a known fact, Little Paw was Mary's favorite.

I would hang out with Thor, and my boys were always there, asking questions about my life, where I had been, what I'd done. Murphy would always respond with why. "Why did you do it that way? Why did you get treated that way? Why are some people like that?" Oh, he was a handful alright.

I visited with Lady, at least once a day also, reassuring her all was right with the world again.

Thor on the other hand was on the alert all the time. Oh yes, happy with his best friend back home, thrilled with his role as an uncle to the young cats, but sensing something was not quite right with his world. His foreboding feeling came to light three days after I came home, when all hell broke loose.

Chapter 41

One thing Zane didn't take into account in his plan was the beast inside his breed. Although they could stalk and kill prey more silently than any other land predator in the Eastern United States except for wolves, the instinct to howl themselves into kill frenzy, prior to the hunt, was overwhelming. When the dark of a moonless night arrived, the freedom of the hunt came over them and they roared their intentions to the world. Then, deathly silent, they took off on a smooth, quiet, loping run towards the farm.

The howls did not go unnoticed at the farm. A combination of my arrival and the uneasy feeling of being watched from the woods had made Thor's decision to sleep outside at night a necessity instead of a choice. His job was to protect what was his, and it had become extremely important to him to be able to smell the outside air, listen for any dangerously different noises or sense vibrations as quickly as possible. Lying out by his doghouse, he heard the howls, and sensed the vibrations of the running beast echoing through the ground.

I was in the barn, watching the young cats and talking with Cally in chirps and body language, telling her of my adventures. The girls were cleaning each other in a semi half asleep state getting ready for the night's sleep, and the boys were hunting a mouse which had crossed their path a few minutes before the howls started.

When I heard the coyotes yelling their war cries, I instinctively knew something was not right and we were in great danger. Jumping up, body on full alert, tail and jowls bushed out to twice their size, I howled to everyone to hide and ran outside.

Cally was shocked at my actions, considering we knew the pack of coyotes had been in the area for awhile, were cautious during the day in our wanderings, and safe in the barn at night, so why my violent reaction now? Then, she too, realized the howls had been different, more violent, and more vicious and she reacted. She demanding her children stay in the barn, securing them in a hiding place in the loft behind bales of hay. She commanded them to stay put no matter what they heard, she ran off to find me.

At first they listened to her, but Murphy, lying next to his brother, puffed up, eyes wide, started thinking. "Smokey, something is terribly wrong and I think our mama is facing a great danger running out there with our poppa. We can't let them do it alone."

Smoky, listening to the outside noises, cleaning his paws, and feeling strange vibrations vibrating through his fur, finally agreed. "I think you're right. Something is wrong. Let's go."

Standing up, stretching their muscular bodies, and testing their claws, they took off, slowly at first, then faster until they were on a full run. The girls looked at one another and Queenie demanded the girls stay right there in the barn. Little Paw argued, meowing, "Mama might need us."

Queenie hissed her command again, and finally, the girls settled down, waiting and fretting the whole time.

Chapter 42

Thor heard the coyotes before he saw them. They were coming in slow and close to the ground, then faster until they were at a full run towards the yard.

He barked an incessant warning to the barn and house. Harry came to the door to see what the danger was, saw the movement in the woods and knew instantly Thor was in great danger and ran for his 12 gauge Winchester pump action shotgun. Grabbing a handful of super X high brass game loads out of a box, he ran for the door, flung it open and loaded on the run. Mary grabbed the box of shells; the baseball bat Harry kept by the door and out she flew right on his heels.

Once at a full run, the wolves were visible to Thor. To his dismay, he saw 4 of them coming in at 3 directions. He knew, at once, what their plan was and was positive there were more lurking out there. Once these four jumped the fence, one would get between him and the house, surrounding him on all four sides, and attack at once.

Growling wildly, teeth barred, ears back, hair up, muscles taut, Thor readied himself for the attack.

As he expected, all four jumped the fence at once, teeth fully exposed, drooling saliva, growling now, with one thought in mind, "Kill."

The coyote that circled, who came in between Thor and the house, was a slight bit slower, so as to gain an advantage, while the other three hit him at once. As she sprung toward the melee, Harry raised the shotgun and fired, the shell hitting her in the back just under the shoulder blade and she dropped like a dead weight, screaming in both anger and pain. It was Teeya, Zane's mate.

Harry pumped the shotgun for a second round and realized the other three were on Thor in a jumbled mass of bodies. If he fired, he might hit the dog. He lowered the rifle and ran in closer.

Thor, an intelligent animal, well fed and with a muscled body, slightly larger then a coyote, went into a life and death battle of both wits and brawn. One coyote landed on his back, trying to bring him down, so the second one could get to his throat. The third hit him in the hindquarter, He was expecting the fourth to attack, knowing it would try and get under him to rip and tear his belly. He heard the rifle shot, the coyote scream, and knew the farmer was there and the belly attack would not come. The thought gave him an additional adrenalin boost and confidence so he could win this death fight, or at least take down a couple himself before dying.

With all the strength available to him, he reached behind, grabbed the one coyote by the leg and pulled, shaking his head violently. It worked and the animal lost its hold on his back, and its balance, and fell to the ground. From the violence of the blow and the way the animal fell, a cracking, popping noise was heard by Thor, and he knew the animal had broken a leg.

Along with the body came a chunk out of Thor's neck in its mouth, and he started bleeding profusely from the wound. The coyote in front smelled blood and possibly victory and hit Thor, in the throat area, hoping it would be the death blow. At the same time, Thor whirled his head around readying himself for the attack, and his collar chain hit the coyote's teeth, and deflected the bite. In that split second of surprise, Thor lunged and bit deep and as hard as he could into his enemy's neck. The coyote screamed out while blood pumped out of his neck everywhere. Then Thor went down.

The third coyote had ripped through Thor's leg, exposing muscle tissue, and as Thor had lunged for the other's throat, between the weight of the animal on his rear and the damaged leg muscle wound, he lost his balance and could not regain it.

At the same time another coyote was leaping through the air from the other side of the fence, and Harry was ready. Second shot, and another dead on hit.

Mary saw Thor go down, and screamed. Wielding the baseball bat, she ran up behind Thor and whacked the coyote that had latched on to Thor's leg. She hit him once, twice. It was so surprised it let go of Thor and turned to lunge at her. She brought the bat down again and this time smacked the coyote right in the side of the mouth, spittle, blood and teeth spraying all over the ground. The animal screamed, then growled and ran, jumping the fence, howling in pain.

It was suddenly deathly quiet. It seemed, the battle was over. Mary dropped the bat and went to Thor's head, put it in her lap and cooed to him, yelling for Harry to come and help her.

Harry lowered the shotgun and walked to her side, laid his gun down next to his dog, and felt him over with his hands. Thor was still alive. He had a nasty gash on his neck. He had lost a lot of blood from it, but it had started to clot. This was a good thing. An artery had not been severed. Then he looked at Thor's leg. The bone had been shattered, and the muscle torn and exposed. He hoped his boy wouldn't lose his leg, but it didn't look good at all.

Lifting the exhausted animal, Harry carried him back to the house. "Get the shotgun Mary, please." Mary picked up the shotgun and the baseball bat and followed Harry into the house.

Zane had waited in the shadows watching all this go down. When his mate was hit by the bullet and fell, something snapped in his brain. He now wanted to kill the feral and all his family, including the humans. This war was not over and tonight they would all die.

Chapter 43

I arrived at the fence just as everything was happening in the yard. As I jumped to the top of the fence, I saw the four coyotes jump the fence and attack Thor. I saw the farmer shoot the two, Mary hitting the one with the bat, and Thor go down, all of it.

In reality, it all happened so fast, but to me it felt like slow motion and there was nothing I could do. Then out of my peripheral vision, I saw Zane and another two skulking in the woods, hiding in the dark. Harry had already picked Thor up, turned and walked back to the house with Mary following. The human's night vision was not as acute as mine, and I knew they didn't see the others crouching in the shadows. I let out an ear piercing howl, screaming for them to turn around.

Mary heard my danger call as did all else close by. She turned, looked, but kept walking into the house. Harry had already entered with Thor in his arms and I did not know if he had heard my call or not.

It had gotten Zane's total attention, and his head whirled around. Both he and I stared each other directly in the eyes. Zane's lip curled with a deep throated growl. If coyotes could smile, it was definitely an evil grin. "I've got you now. You're mine little feral. I've waited a long time for this pleasure."

At about the same time, Zane saw the movement coming from the barn. "His family of feral delicacy. My pack eats tonight."

He turned to the other two "Your dinner awaits. The others are in the bush behind the feral. You can have them, but remember this one is mine. Go!"

Zane leaped for the fence, aiming straight for me. I was a little faster then he expected, jumped off the fence, across the yard, leaped up and over the other side and raced back around the fencing through the woods to where I had started.

Zane, actually felt like he could taste the blood of the feral. Jumping over the fence, he landed where I had hit the ground a second before. Rage engulfed him when he realized he had missed me by a hair, and no longer was the silent hunter. He let out a howl that sent shivers of fear down the spines of all living creatures within hearing distance. Across the yard he went and over the other side, growling, spittle flying, and kept on going for a distance, then stopped short. Looking around wild eyed, he came to the conclusion that something was wrong. He no longer could smell me, nor did he hear me running.

All in the house heard the coyote, including Lady. She actually couldn't hear him, but felt the vibration very soundly and sensed the evil within it. Jumping to her window, she looked out and saw Cally in the sunflower patch, while, two coyotes were circling for attack. She screamed, a high pitched yowl, all the hair on her body stood up, her tail bushed and she started to shake. "Help her, help her."

Mary looked out the window to see what had scared her so much, and she saw them. Not only was Cally out there, but Smokey and Murphy were coming up behind the coyotes, low to the ground and in an attack stance as if they were hunting mice or birds.

"Oh my God, no" she yelled as she dropped Lady on the couch, turned and ran for the door.

Harry had been on the phone calling a couple of his farm employees to help clean up the mess of animals in the backyard, and to show up with rifle or shotgun. He had all intentions of a coyote hunt at first light the next day.

"What's the matter? Mary, what is it?"

All Mary could say as she ran for the door, "They're back, and the cats are in danger."

He grabbed his shotgun as he ran out the door after his wife, and suddenly realized he had no ammunition. He ran back to where he kept it and it was missing. "What the hell." Mary must have taken it with her when they first were out there, and he ran after her yelling "Dam it, where's the ammo?"

Mary heard him and reached into her pocket only to realize it wasn't there. "I must have dropped it," stopped to look around the yard, and spotted the box of shells. . Running for it, she heard a growl and looked up. Standing a few feet from where the shells were there was the largest, most evil looking coyote she had ever seen.

Harry stopped also, and yelled to Mary, "Don't move," but she was already frozen, fear engulfing her like a physical entity, trying to smother her. She felt like she couldn't breathe.

Helplessness passed over Harry for a brief second, and then he started waving his arms, yelling at the coyote, moving swiftly and meaningfully in its direction.

The coyote held its ground, growling back, all the while thinking out its options. "If the gun was loaded, he would have fired. This man is the one who killed Teeya. I vowed vengeance for her, his mate must die." Lowering himself in position of attack, he heard the familiar cry of the feral.

He looked past Mary, and saw me up on the fence where I was before, yowling at him in a loud and deep war cry. His went totally insane, sighted in on me, forgetting Mary, and flew up, past her and at the fence.

Again, I was faster then him and moved like lightening. Off the fence into the woods I ran, faster and faster, until I felt I was flying, but he was catching up to me. His size and running stride was much greater then mine and I knew eventually he would have me in his jaws.

Chapter 44

When Harry saw the coyote charge towards his wife, he screamed, " Jesus, Nooooo," and ran to get between her and the animal. It flew past them, and Harry spun around and saw me.

"Jesus," the dam cat saved you. It made itself bait."

Hugging Mary, he said "Go into the house and stay there. With that he grabbed the box of shotgun shells off the ground, shoving as many as he could in pockets, jumped the fence and took off in the direction of the me and coyote.

It was dark outside the compound with no moon for light. It was a clear night though, and the stars gave some shadows to the woods. Harry knew his property quite well, and followed the coyote easily, both by memory and the sound of the animal.

Zane, in his chase after me, was no longer the silent stalker, but making a lot of noise now. Head down, eyes squinted, teeth bared, Zane lunged for me and with one strike, had me in his jaws. He lifted his head and shook me unmercifully at the stars and then dropped me to the ground. Lifting his head high, he howled at the sky, "Victory, finally, victory is mine."

I hit the ground like a bag of sodden garbage. I was shaken so hard, I felt as if every fiber of my being had become unglued and couldn't see straight or even think straight. I felt no pain, but knew I was bleeding, but did not know from where. All I could think of was. " I lost. My family is not safe. They'll all die like me."

Zane stopped howling and looked down at me. He growled, "I no longer am in a hurry my furry friend. It is enjoyable to watch you suffer for a while before I kill you and eat you."

But, Zane in his gloating and omnipotent ego, had waited too long. Chasing me, he no longer was the silent stalker of his prey, but quite noisy in his closing run, easy to follow.

When he raised his head to the sky, Harry spotted his silhouette against the star filled sky. Stopping he loaded the Winchester, and eased himself towards the coyote.

Zane, lost in his reverie, did not feel the presence of danger until the farmer was almost on top of him. He whirled around, eyes wide from surprise, snarled and jumped at Harry.

Harry fired, and the shell hit the animal in the shoulder, knocking him down, Regaining balance, Zane took off towards the woods howling in both pain and frustration. Harry pumped the shotgun and fired the second shell in the direction of the running canine, but didn't know if he hit it again or not. Then he noticed me, a black ball of fur, trying to crawl away.

I was still alive, but just barely. The pain started coming in excruciating waves now. I was going into a state of shock and my body was becoming catatonic. The last thing I remember for a long time was the feeling of being picked up and being placed in a warm, dark place.

Harry had gently picked me up, and placed me inside his shirt next to his warm chest, shouldered the shotgun and made the hike back to the farm.

Chapter 45

Ranger Dan had been on rounds in the area of the farm this particular day. He had been visiting a fire tower in a nearby mountain, taking inventory of equipment and surveying the land for any unusual smoke activity, and leaving later then he had planned. It was dark out by now, and he was concentrating on the bumpy ride down from the mountain in his jeep. It wasn't more then a rutted dirt patch leading into the road to the farm, just before it intersected with the main road. Going slow, he heard the rifle shots and a man yelling. Sound travels in the quiet dark mountains, and he heard the distinct words "Jesus no!" When he reached the farm road he turned in to see if anyone needed help.

Cally heard the ruckus coming from the yard, and started to run reaching the sunflower patch, and sensed before actually seeing the two coyotes moving in her direction. She laid down in the stalks, ears back, and froze like a statue hoping beyond hope that they would not see or sense her, relieved that her children were safely tucked away in the barn.

`Murphy and Smokey also heard the ruckus coming from the yard, and saw, first, the coyotes prowling towards the sunflower patch, and then their mama cat, crouched down.

"We've gotta do something Smokey. Mama doesn't stand a chance."

"I know Murph, but what? We need a plan."

"There's no time. We must stop them, somehow," and Murphy started moving in behind the stalking coyotes.

As they got closer to mama, Murphy realized what was going to happen. The beasts were closing in on the kill, their teeth bared, low growls coming from their throats and heading straight towards her. Without thinking, Murphy stood up and screamed "Come and get me you devils. You want cat, here I am."

The coyotes stopped, turned their heads in his direction, sneered and the one said, "Oh my, a tender morsel for the taking." He turned and sighted in on the noisy feral.

Murphy was a fast cat. Built like his distant cousin, the Cheetah, with a lean body and longer hind legs than front, he could run and leap as swiftly as the wind. He took off running with the coyote right behind him. The animal lunged and was totally surprised that he missed the first time, teeth gnashing together empty. He lunged again and this time he caught Murphy by his long tail. The coyote whipped him in the air and swung him around, but at the same time a rifle shot pierced the air, hitting the coyote smack in the middle of the chest and he fell with a resounding thump.

The falling coyote is probably what saved Murphy's life. It all happened so quickly that it didn't have a chance of smashing him onto the ground, and the cat fell with the canine.

The other coyote was now sighting in on Cally. She was crouched in the grasses, hissing venomously now, fluffed out as much as nature would allow.

Smokey, with his dark gray, almost totally black coloring, was almost invisible in the night sky. He had no problem slinking around the coyote until he was right next to his mama. He rose up, his body and tail also fluffed out, and with his long hair he looked almost three times his size. Hissing like a steam train under full power, he was a commanding sight that turned the coyote's attention totally on him.

The coyote lunged for him. Smokey, not as fast in running would have made a great prize fighter. In months of playing games with his brother, he had become very adept at side stepping and weaving away from his brother's blows, and it became a life saving tactic. Weaving and sidestepping from the drooling mouth and razor sharp teeth, he avoided a death blow. The coyote caught him on the ear and ripped a piece of it off. Blood started spurting everywhere which brought the canine into a full feeding frenzy, and Smokey knew the next blow might be his death.

Cally sprung into action, and hit the coyote on the side of the face near his eye. She bit down, grabbed deep into his skin with all four claws, one of which hooked into the eye. The coyote reared up, howling in anger and pain, and shook his head wildly, but Cally, with every fiber of her feline body, hung on, digging her claws all the way to their ends by her pads.

Then another rifle shot went off. The coyote totally startled by the sound of a weapon, turned tail and ran, while the shot whizzed over his head. Cally let go, but one of her nails got stuck and trapped her on the fleeing animal. She yanked with all her might to get free and suddenly she was falling. She spun around in mid air and landed on all four paws, and felt a sharp brief pain in one front foot. She looked down and a spot on her foot was trickling blood. She had left her nail in the coyote and had de-clawed herself permanently of the one claw. Limping back she found Smokey, with a blood filled face and half an ear, but the battle was over. The coyotes were gone.

Danny had shown up in his jeep moments after Harry took off after Zane. His first view of the yard looked to him like a war zone of animal carcass. Then he looked up and saw Mary running towards him like a wild woman. She screamed, "The coyotes have them trapped between here and the barn."

He didn't know who "them" were, but realized it was serious. He grabbed his loaded rifle out the vehicle, jumped the fence and headed in the direction of the barn. He spotted the first coyote with the cat in his mouth, raised the rifle and fired. The shot connected right with the coyote's chest and it fell. No noise, just a phish of air and a thud. He spotted the other one racing off into the woods and fired. He knew he missed it, but doubted it would be back soon.

Chapter 46

One Month later

Sleeping on the back of the couch under the cold light of a winter day coming through the window, with Lady snuggled up next to me, I dreamed about running free and chasing butterflies. The warm grasses full of dew under my feet, and mama watching and laughing. I guess I was twitching and moving around quite a bit, because I woke to Lady, softly meowing my name, licking my face. I looked down and Thor was laying on the floor beneath us, thumping his tail and looking up at us.

The coyote had not only broken Thor's leg, but had shattered the bone in the lower thigh area. It had to be reconstructed with pins in order to save it. He also suffered some nerve damage to the leg and would always walk with a limp. His leg was still in a cast, and would be for another month. He was healing well, and adjusted to hobbling around with it. The only thing that drove him nuts was the itch under the cast. So much so, that he had to wear a neck shield so he wouldn't scratch and bite at the cast.

He hated it so much, that Mary took to removing it for a while each day, and would put it back on when he started his biting and scratching at the cast. He was smart enough to realize if he didn't touch the cast, he could go without the neck shield, so he tried hard not to touch the leg. Every once in a while though, the itch and irritation got so strong, he couldn't help himself, and he'd start biting the cast, trying to get at the itch, and then Mary would put the hated shield back on his neck again.

The shield was off then, and he had been resting peacefully, but the irritating itch was getting to him again. He first started licking the leg just above the cast, and then started nibbling and then chewing at the top of it. My heart felt pain for him, and I slipped off the couch and down to the floor with my friend.

"Thor, if you get caught chewing on the cast, the neck shield will go back on again."

"Can't help it Squeaky. It's so itchy it drives me nuts."

"Let me help." I lay down next to him and started licking the leg just above the cast, trying to get my tongue down under it enough to help with the itch. Cats have such rough tongues, and I knew the sandpaper feel might help ease the irritation, even if just a little. It seemed to help and he laid his head back down and thumped his tail in a thank you. The workout tired me though, and I felt myself snuggling next to his warm body and started to fall asleep again. I drifted off to my memories of that night when we fought the coyotes, which seemed so long ago.

I remembered when the coyote finally caught me and wrapped his jaws around my body. I could smell his vile breath, his hot, wet mouth and the grip of his teeth. He shook me so hard that it felt as if my mind was being whirled through a blender and my body was being turned into liquid mush. When he flung me to the ground I felt as if the only thing holding me together was my skin, otherwise I would have been a dark wet puddle of blood and broken insides pouring out all over the grasses. I don't remember much of what happened after that for quite some time. Just vague feelings of hearing a loud pop, then being picked up and tucked away in a warm soft place. I could hear a heartbeat, felt safe and thought that my mama had come and tucked me under her warm furry belly. I learned later what had happened.

Harry had shot the coyote, picked me up, tucked me inside his shirt and carried me back to the house. Danny, the ranger, killed one of the other two coyotes and scared the third one off, saving my family. Cally lost a claw, the girls were fine, but Murphy and Smokey had suffered some injuries.

Smokey had lost part of an ear. The doctor stitched part of it back to his head and saved it, but the tip was gone. After that, he always looked a little lopsided when he would look at you.

Murphy lost part of his tail. The coyote had bit about a third of it completely off. Afterward, everyone started calling him "Stubby." Oh, he acted so angry when anyone called him that, but I knew deep down inside, Murphy was very proud of his nickname.

I stretched in my reverie, flexed my claws, and chuckled a bit. Not because of what happened to them, but because, both Smokey and Murphy earned those scars, and would walk proudly the rest of their lives knowing they saved their mama. I felt great pride in knowing I had sired such strong and brave children.

Then I thought about Thor, and twitched a bit in my dreamlike state. A sad moan softly escaped my lips. It saddened me because I felt responsible for leading those monsters back to my home. Having a limp and nerve damage to his leg for the rest of his days was not what he deserved. Thor's courage proved what a mighty warrior he was with a heart as big as the sky.

Then I sat up, and shuffled back to the couch and managed to jump up on the soft cushions and found a comfortable position to lay my body down again. I felt so old. When the day got bitter cold and the sky filled with snow, my body ached so badly and I thought about myself and the things I did remember from those dark days after the war.

The next thing I remember after the warm soft place with the heartbeat that made me feel like my mama's warm underbelly, I was on a table with tubes sticking out of my body, and a female voice saying, "Easy boy, you're in the hospital and we're helping you." At first, I thought I jumped up and started to run, but the only thing that was happening, was my legs were shuffling back and forth on the table and I wasn't going anywhere. I howled out in fear and then remembered nothing for a while longer.

Three days later, I came back to life, really awake for the first time in a week. I was in pain, every fiber of my body ached, but I was alive and hungry. The Veterinarian explained what was going on with me to Mary and Harry. Little did she realize, but I understood everything she was saying. Seems I had no broken bones, but all my muscles and internal organs were severely bruised from the shaking. Luckily, I was a healthy young cat with a good bone structure.

She went on to say, "Cats don't have bones as rigid as some mammals. They're more resilient and flexible which enables them to look like they can distort their bodies and can actually bend the bones without breaking. He's a very well muscled and strong little cat. This is what probably saved him. The negative side is we don't know if there was any permanent damage to his organs from the violent shaking, it will take time for him to heal inside completely. He could develop neurological problems in balance, kidney problems or several other conditions including bone spurs that could cause issues. Only time will tell. Meanwhile, take him home, and keep him quiet, warm, and well fed. I'll give you some pain pills and antibiotics to keep him calm and ward off any infection, and we'll see him in three weeks."

So, I went home to a pampered world. It was winter now, and I was confined to the house. No more barn or outside for awhile. I didn't mind. Lady was my constant companion, and Cally and the children would come and visit on a daily basis. Smokey and Murphy healed beautifully from their injuries, and were back to their old ways. Murphy would always be a hellion getting into all kinds of mischief and Smokey remained his protector and companion through it all.

Me, well I got a bit more gray hairs mixed in my black sheen, I was slower moving and slept more soundly that ever before. I became more in tune with my ancestry, and the memories that all cats share of the wild. My dreams were full of them. The big cats of the jungle, the dessert and the mountains. I could feel the pull of that freedom, the hunt, and the taste of raw meat. I was just thankful for this knowledge, knowing this is why I and other cats survived the trials of life. I learned how to love, hate, trust and distrust. To recognize the good, bad and ugly in all species including humankind without judging each one the same. I grew into an animal that cared and trusted, but at the same time cautious of who or what I gave love and affection. Without eons of programmed instinct, I would not have survived and I know I will heal completely and move on to more adventures.

Printed in the United States
By Bookmasters